"Keiko, a defiantly oddball 36-year-old woman, has worked in a
dead-end job as a convenience store cashier in Tokyo for half her
life. She lives alone and has never been in a romantic relationship,
or even had sex. And she is perfectly happy with all of it . . . Written
in plain-spoken prose, the slim volume focuses on a character who
in many ways personifies a demographic panic in Japan."

—*New York Times* (profile)

"Brilliant, witty, and sweet in ways that recall *Amélie* and *Shop-
girl* . . . Murata's sparkly writing and knack for odd, beautiful
details are totally her own."

—*Vogue*, "13 Books to Thrill, Entertain,
and Sustain You This Summer"

"Alienation gets deliciously perverse treatment in *Convenience
Store Woman* . . . Murata celebrate[s] the quiet heroism of women
who accept the cost of being themselves." —NPR's *Fresh Air*

"I picked up this novel on a trip to Japan and couldn't put it down. A haunting, dark, and often hilarious take on society's expectations of the single woman. As an extra bonus, it totally transformed my experience of going to convenience stores in Tokyo."

—Elif Batuman, author of *The Idiot*

"*Convenience Store Woman* is a mighty fine book, completely charming. Sayaka Murata is a wonderful writer."

—Rabih Alameddine, author of
An Unnecessary Woman

"Instructions: Open book. Consume contents. Feel charmed, disturbed, and weirdly in love. Do not discard."

—Jade Chang, author of *The Wangs Vs. the World*

"This book is not only readable, it is fun, thought-provoking, and at times outrageous and outrageously funny. It is sure to be a standout of the year."

—Weike Wang, author of *Chemistry*

"This novel made me laugh. It was the first time for me to laugh in this way: it was absurd, comical, cute . . . audacious, and precise. It was overwhelming."   —Hiromi Kawakami, author of
The Nakano Thrift Shop

"Sayaka Murata's brilliant *Convenience Store Woman* can be read as a meditation on the world of personal branding . . . It's a sign of excellent literature to be able to effortlessly hold up multiple interpretations at once. Murata's book is no exception: It's all of these things while also rendering an artful grotesque of modern personal branding."   —*The Millions*

CONVENIENCE
STORE
WOMAN

CONVENIENCE STORE WOMAN

SAYAKA MURATA

Translated from the Japanese by
GINNY TAPLEY TAKEMORI

Grove Press
New York

Original published as *Konbini ningen*. Japanese edition published by
Bungeishunju Ltd., Tokyo. English language translation rights reserved
to Grove Atlantic, Inc. under license granted by Sakaya Murata arranged
with Bungeishunju Ltd. through The English Agency (Japan) Ltd.

Published simultaneously in Canada
Printed in Canada

First Grove Atlantic hardcover edition: June 2018
First Grove Atlantic paperback edition: September 2019

This book was set in 11 point Berling
by Alpha Design & Composition of Pittsfield, NH.

Library of Congress Cataloging-in-Publication data is available for this title.

ISBN 978-0-8021-2962-8
eISBN 978-0-8021-6580-0

Grove Press
an imprint of Grove Atlantic
154 West 14th Street
New York, NY 10011

JAPANFOUNDATION 国際交流基金
Grove Atlantic gratefully acknowledges the support from
the Japan Foundation for this publication.

Distributed by Publishers Group West

groveatlantic.com

23 24 25   13 12

CONVENIENCE
STORE
WOMAN

A convenience store is a world of sound. From the tinkle of the door chime to the voices of TV celebrities advertising new products over the in-store cable network, to the calls of the store workers, the beeps of the bar code scanner, the rustle of customers picking up items and placing them in baskets, and the clacking of heels walking around the store. It all blends into the convenience store sound that ceaselessly caresses my eardrums.

I hear the faint rattle of a new plastic bottle rolling into place as a customer takes one out of the refrigerator, and look up instantly. A cold drink is often the last item customers take before coming to the checkout till, and my body responds automatically to the sound. I see a woman holding a bottle of mineral water while perusing the desserts and look back down.

As I arrange the display of newly delivered rice balls, my body picks up information from the multitude of sounds around the store. At this time of day, rice balls, sandwiches, and salads are what sell best. Another part-timer, Sugawara, is over at the other side of the store checking off items with a handheld scanner. I continue laying out the pristine, machine-made food neatly on the shelves of the cold display: in the middle I place two rows of the new flavor, spicy cod roe with cream cheese, alongside two rows of the store's best-selling flavor, tuna mayonnaise, and then I line the less popular dry bonito shavings in soy sauce flavor next to those. Speed is of the essence, and I barely use my head as the rules ingrained in me issue instructions directly to my body.

Alerted by a faint clink of coins I turn and look over at the cash register. It's a sound I'm sensitive to, since customers who come just to buy cigarettes or a newspaper often jingle coins in their hand or pocket. And yes: as I'd thought, a man with a can of coffee in one hand, the other hand in his pocket, is approaching the till. I quickly move through the store, slide behind the counter, and stand at the ready so as not to keep him waiting.

"Irasshaimasé! Good morning, sir."

I bow and take the can of coffee he holds out to me.

"Oh, and a pack of Marlboro Menthol Lights."

"Right away, sir." I take out a pack of the cigarettes and scan the bar code. "Please confirm your age on the touch screen."

As he does so, I notice him glance at the hot-food cabinet. I could ask him whether he'd like anything else, but when a customer appears to be dithering over whether or not to buy something, I make a point of taking a step back and waiting.

"And a corn dog."

"Right away, sir. Thank you."

I disinfect my hands with alcohol, open the hot cabinet, and take out a corn dog.

"Shall I put the hot food and cold drink in separate bags?"

"Oh no, don't bother. Together's fine."

I put the can of coffee, cigarettes, and corn dog into a small-size bag. Until then the man had been jingling the coins in his pocket, but now he suddenly moves his hand to his breast pocket as though something has just occurred to him. Instantly I deduce that he will use electronic money.

"I'll pay by Suica."

"Certainly, sir. Please touch your card here."

I automatically read the customer's minutest movements and gaze, and my body acts reflexively in response. My ears and eyes are important sensors to catch their every move and desire. Taking the utmost care not to cause the customer any discomfort by observing him or her too closely, I swiftly move my hands according to whatever signals I pick up.

"Your receipt, sir. Thank you for your custom!"

"Thanks," he says, taking his receipt and leaving.

"I'm sorry to have kept you waiting," I say with a bow to the woman next in the queue. "Irasshaimasé. Good morning!"

The morning period is passing normally in the brightly lit box of the convenience store, I feel. Visible outside the windows, polished free of fingerprints, are the figures of people rushing by. It is the start of another day, the time when the world wakes up and the cogs of society begin to move. I am one of those cogs, going round and round. I have become a functioning part of the world, rotating in the time of day called morning.

I am just running to put out more rice balls when our supervisor, Mrs. Izumi, calls out to me. "Miss Furukura, how many five-thousand-yen notes are there left in that till?"

"Um, only two."

"Oh dear, there must have been a lot of customers paying with ten-thousand-yen notes. There aren't many left in the safe either. I'd better go to the bank this morning, once the rush and deliveries have calmed down."

"Yes, thank you!"

Mrs. Izumi is a casual worker about the same age as me, but the night shift has been so short of staff lately that the store manager has been doing nights and putting her in charge during the day, as though she were a regular staff member sent from head office.

"Okay then, I'll go for change around ten o'clock. And while I'm thinking about it, there happens to be a special order for sushi pockets today, so please keep an eye out for the customer when he comes to collect it."

"I will!"

I look at the clock: almost nine thirty. The morning rush is nearly over, and I have to finish dealing with the delivery and start preparing for the lunchtime rush. I stretch my back and go out into the store to finish putting out the rice balls.

* * *

The time before I was reborn as a convenience store worker is somewhat unclear in my memory. I was born into a normal family and lovingly brought up in a normal suburban residential area. But everyone thought I was a rather strange child.

There was the time when I was in nursery school, for example, when I saw a dead bird in the park. It was small, a pretty blue, and must have been someone's pet. It lay there with its neck twisted and eyes closed, and the other children were all standing around it crying. One girl started to ask: "What should we—" But before she could finish I snatched it up and ran over to the bench where my mother was chatting with the other mothers.

"What's up, Keiko? Oh! A little bird . . . where did it come from I wonder?" she said gently, stroking my hair. "The poor thing. Shall we make a grave for it?"

"Let's eat it!" I said.

"What?"

"Daddy likes yakitori, doesn't he? Let's grill it and have it for dinner!"

She looked at me, startled. Thinking she hadn't heard properly, I repeated what I'd said, this time clearly enunciating my words. The mother sitting next to her gaped at me, her eyes, nostrils, and mouth forming perfect O's. She looked so comical I almost burst out laughing. But then I saw her staring at the bird in my hand and I realized that one of these little birds probably wouldn't be enough for Daddy.

"Shall I get some more?" I asked, glancing at two or three other birds strutting around.

"Keiko!" my mother exclaimed reprovingly, finally coming to her senses. "Let's make a grave for Mr. Budgie and bury him. Look, everyone's crying. His friends must be sad he died. The poor little thing!"

"But it's *dead*. Let's eat it!"

My mother was speechless, but I was captivated by the vision of my parents and little sister happily tucking in around the dinner table. My father was always saying how tasty yakitori was, and what was that if not grilled bird? There were lots more there in the park, so all we had to do was catch some and take them home. I couldn't understand why should we bury the bird instead of eating it.

"Look how cute little Mr. Budgie is!" my mother said earnestly. "Let's make a grave for him over there, and everyone can lay flowers on it."

And that's what we did. Everyone was crying for the poor dead bird as they went around murdering flowers, plucking their stalks, exclaiming, "What lovely flowers! Little Mr. Budgie will definitely be pleased." They looked so bizarre I thought they must all be out of their minds.

We buried the bird in a hole dug on the other side of a fence with a sign that said KEEP OUT and placed the flower corpses on top of it. Someone brought an ice lolly stick from the trash can to use as a grave marker.

"Poor little bird. It's so sad, isn't it Keiko?" my mother kept murmuring, as if trying to convince me. But I didn't think it was sad at all.

There were many other similar incidents. There was also that big commotion soon after I started primary school, when some boys started fighting during the break time.

The other kids started wailing, "Get a teacher!" and "Someone stop them!" And so I went to the tool shed, took out a spade, ran over to the unruly boys, and bashed one of them over the head. Everyone started screaming as he fell down clutching his skull. Seeing as he'd stopped moving, my attention turned to the other

CONVENIENCE STORE WOMAN 9

boy, and I raised the spade again. "Keiko-chan, stop! Please stop!" the girls shouted at me tearfully.

Some teachers came over and, dumbfounded, demanded I explain myself.

"Everyone was saying to stop them, so that's what I did."

Violence was wrong, the bewildered teachers told me in confusion.

"But everyone was saying to stop Yamazaki-kun and Aoki-kun fighting! I just thought that would be the quickest way to do it," I explained patiently. Why on earth were they so angry? I just didn't get it.

They held a teacher's meeting, and my mother was called to the school. Seeing her bowing to the teachers, apologizing over and over, her face strangely serious, I finally realized that maybe I shouldn't have done what I did, but I still couldn't understand why.

It was the same that time when our young class teacher became hysterical and began bawling and hitting her desk furiously with the attendance register, and everyone started crying. She wouldn't calm down even when everyone started begging, "We're sorry, Miss!" "Please stop, Miss!" So in order to shut her up I ran over and yanked her skirt and knickers down. She was so shocked she burst into tears, but at least she became quiet.

The teacher from the next class came running in and asked me what had happened, so I explained that I'd once seen on TV how a grown-up woman who was all worked up went quiet after someone took her clothes off. But then they held another teachers' meeting and my mother was summoned again.

"I wonder why you can't understand, Keiko . . ." she muttered helplessly on the way home, hugging me to her. It seemed I'd done something wrong again, but I couldn't for the life of me understand what was the problem.

My parents were at a loss what to do about me, but they were as affectionate to me as ever. I'd never meant to make them sad or have to keep apologizing for things I did, so I decided to keep my mouth shut as best I could outside home. I would no longer do anything of my own accord, and would either just mimic what everyone else was doing, or simply follow instructions.

After this, the adults seemed relieved when I didn't say a single word more than necessary or act on my own initiative. But as I got older, being so quiet apparently became a problem in itself. As far as I was concerned, though, keeping my mouth shut was the most sensible approach to getting by in life. Even when my teachers wrote in my school report that I should make more friends and play outside more, I doggedly refused to say anything more than absolutely necessary.

My little sister, who is two years younger than me, was a normal child. Even so, she never tried to avoid me; indeed, she adored me. Unlike me she was always being told off for silly little things, and whenever this happened I would go up to mother and ask her why she was so angry. This generally put an end to the lecture, and my sister always thanked me for it as if she thought I were protecting her. It also helped that I wasn't all that interested in sweets and toys and would often give them to her, and so she was always hanging around me.

My family always loved and cherished me, and that's why they were so worried and wanted to cure me. I recall hearing my parents discussing how to do this, and wondered what it was about me that needed correcting. My father once drove me some distance to another town to meet a therapist. The therapist immediately assumed there must be some problem at home, but really there wasn't. My father, a bank clerk, was a mild and steady type, while my mother was kind if a little timid, and my little sister was really fond of me. "For the time being, shower her with affection and let's see how things go" was the bland conclusion, and so my parents assiduously brought me up with loving care.

I didn't make any friends at school, but I wasn't particularly picked on or bullied, and I managed to get myself through elementary and secondary without saying anything uncalled for.

I didn't even change after graduating from high school and going on to university. I basically spent my free time alone, and didn't talk to anyone in private at all. I never repeated the kind of trouble I'd caused in primary school, but still my parents worried that I wouldn't survive in the real world. And so, believing that I had to be cured, I grew into adulthood.

* * *

The Smile Mart outside Hiiromachi Station opened on May 1, 1998, soon after I started university.

I can still clearly recall the moment I came across the as-yet-unopened store. I'd been to see a Noh performance as part of my coursework and, not having any friends, was making my way home alone when I took a wrong turn and found myself in a completely unfamiliar office district, totally lost.

It occurred to me all of a sudden that the place was deserted. I was alone in a world of graceful white buildings, an artificial scene of paper models. It was Sunday afternoon, and there was no sign of anyone other than me in the street. It was like a ghost town.

Overwhelmed by a sensation of having stumbled into another dimension, I walked quickly through it looking for a metro station. At last I saw a sign and, relieved, was running toward it when I came across the ground floor of a pure white building converted into what looked like an aquarium.

It didn't have a signboard, or anything else other than a notice stuck on the glass window: HIIROMACHI STATION SMILE MART—OPENING SOON! STAFF WANTED. I timidly peeked through the glass. There was nobody there, and it appeared still to be under construction, with plastic coverings on the walls and lines of empty white shelves. It was hard to believe this vacant space would soon be a convenience store.

The allowance I received from home was enough for me to live on, but still I was interested in some part-time work. I made a note of the number, went home, and called the next day. After a brief interview, I was given the job on the spot.

Training would start the following week I was told, and when I headed for the store at the appointed time, I found it looking a little more like a convenience store, now partly stocked, with some stationery, handkerchiefs, and other sundries neatly displayed.

There were some other new employees gathered inside: a girl who appeared to be a student like me, a guy who looked like a typical job-hopper, a slightly older woman, probably a housewife—all in all, fifteen very different-looking people of all ages slouched awkwardly about the store.

Eventually the trainer from head office appeared and handed out uniforms to everyone. I put mine on and tidied myself up according to the checklist stuck on the wall. Once those of us with long hair had tied it back, and all of us had removed watches and any other accessories as instructed, the motley bunch did actually now look like convenience store workers.

First we practiced the various phrases we needed to use in the store. Standing shoulder to shoulder in a line, our backs straight, we lifted the corners of our mouths to match the smiling face in the training poster and in turn called out the stock welcoming phrase: Irasshaimasé!

The male trainer checked each of us one by one, instructing us to try again if our voices were too quiet or our expressions too stiff. "Miss Okamoto, don't be so shy. Smile! Mr. Aizaki, speak up a bit! Try again. Miss Furukura, that's perfect. Nice and spirited—keep it up!"

I was good at mimicking the trainer's examples and the model video he'd shown us in the back room. It was the first time anyone had ever taught me how to accomplish a normal facial expression and manner of speech.

For the two weeks prior to opening, we worked in pairs to role-play dealing with imaginary customers. We practiced looking the customer in the eye, smiling and bowing, cleaning our hands with alcohol before handling items from the hot-food cabinet, putting hot and cold items into separate bags, and sanitary products into paper bags. The money in the till was real so we would become accustomed to handling it, but the receipts were marked TRAINING in big letters, and our "customers" were our fellow uniformed workers, so it was rather like playing at shop.

It was fun to see all kinds of people—from university students and guys who played in bands to job-hoppers, housewives, and kids studying for their high school diploma at night school—don the same uniform and transform into the homogenous being known as a convenience store worker. Once the day's training was over, everyone removed their uniforms and reverted to their original state. It was like changing costumes to become a different creature.

After two weeks of training, at long last opening day arrived. I arrived at the store in the morning to find the empty white shelves now fully stocked, the tightly packed items looking somehow unreal.

Finally, it was time. This is the real thing, I thought to myself as the doors opened. Real customers, not the imaginary ones projected in training. And there were all kinds. Being in an office district, I'd had an image of all our customers in business suits or uniforms, but the people waiting outside appeared to be a group of local residents. I watched on in blank amazement as a little old lady walking with a stick came in first, followed by a long stream of customers clutching discount vouchers for rice balls and lunch boxes.

"Hey, Miss Furukura, don't forget to greet our customers!" the manager prompted me.

"Irasshaimasé!" I blurted out, pulling myself together. "Today we are holding a sale to celebrate opening the store. Please look around!"

Even the set phrases we'd been taught to use sounded completely different now that there were customers in the store.

I never knew customers could be so loud! Their footsteps echoed and voices rang out as they walked around the store, confectionery packs rustling as they tossed them into their baskets, the refrigerator door clunking open and shut as they took out cold drinks. Overwhelmed by the sheer volume, I kept yelling out "Irasshaimasé!" over and over again.

The mountain of food and confectionery that was so perfectly displayed it looked artificial soon crumbled under their hands. The store had looked almost fake, but now under their touch it was being vividly transformed.

The first at the cash register was the same little old lady who had been the first through the door. I stood at the till, mentally running through the manual as she put her basket containing a choux crème, a sandwich, and several rice balls down on the counter.

All the staff behind the counter straightened as she approached. Aware of their eyes on me, I bowed to her the way I'd learned in training.

"Irasshaimasé!" I called out in precisely the same tone as the woman in the training video as I pulled the basket toward me and began scanning the bar codes, just as we'd been taught. The manager stood at my side, briskly placing the products in a plastic bag.

"What time do you open?" she asked.

"Um, today we opened at ten. From now on we'll be open all the time!"

Noting how inept I was at answering questions we hadn't practiced in training, the manager quickly followed up with: "From now on we shall be open twenty-four hours, seven days a week, year-round. Please come and shop here at your convenience."

"Oh my, you're open at night too? And early in the morning?"

"Yes," I told her, nodding.

"How very convenient! It's hard for me to walk with my bad hip, you see. The supermarket is so far away. It's been such a bother," she said, giving me a smile.

"Yes, we'll be open twenty-four hours from now on. Please come at your convenience," I said, echoing the phrases the manager had used.

"That's wonderful. It'll be hard on you store workers, though."

"Thank you!" I said, enthusiastically bowing the way the manager had done.

The woman laughed and said, "Thank *you*, I'll come again," and moved away from the till.

"Well done, Miss Furukura," the manager told me. "That was perfect! You kept your calm, even though it was your first time on the till. Good job, keep it up. Oh look, the next customer!"

I looked around and saw a man approaching with lots of discounted rice balls in his basket. "Irasshaimasé!" I called in exactly the same tone as before and bowed, then took the basket from him.

At that moment, for the first time ever, I felt I'd become a part in the machine of society. *I've been reborn,*

I thought. That day, I actually became a normal cog in society.

*   *   *

The Hiiromachi Station Smile Mart has remained open ever since that day, its lights on without a break. Sometimes I use a calculator to work out the number of hours that have passed since then. The other day, the store was open on May 1 for the nineteenth time, having been open continuously for 157,800 hours. I'm now thirty-six years old, and the convenience-store-worker-me is eighteen. None of the other workers who did their training with me are here anymore, and we're now on our eighth manager. Not a single product on sale in the store at that time is left. But I'm still here.

When I first started here, there was a detailed manual that taught me how to be a store worker, and I still don't have a clue how to be a normal person outside that manual.

Even now my parents indulgently look on as I remain in the same dead-end job. There were times in my twenties that I felt sorry for them and went through the motions of applying for career positions, but having only ever had the same job I rarely even passed the screening selection. And even if I made it to an interview I couldn't explain very well why I had spent so many years working there.

Sometimes I even find myself operating the checkout till in my dreams. I wake up with a start, thinking: *Oh! This new line of crisps is missing a price tag*, or, *We've sold a lot of hot tea, so I'd better restock the display cabinet.* I've also been woken up in the middle of the night by the sound of my own voice calling out: "Irasshaimasé!"

When I can't sleep, I think about the transparent glass box that is still stirring with life even in the darkness of night. That pristine aquarium is still operating like clockwork. As I visualize the scene, the sounds of the store reverberate in my eardrums and lull me to sleep.

When morning comes, once again I'm a convenience store worker, a cog in society. This is the only way I can be a normal person.

* * *

I arrive at the Hiiromachi Station Smile Mart every morning at eight. My shift is from nine, but I come early to have breakfast before starting. I pick up a two-liter bottle of mineral water, select a sandwich or bun close to its sell-by date, pay for them, and take them into the back room to eat.

In the back room, the security camera in the store is relayed on a big screen. This morning Dat-kun, a Vietnamese guy new on the night shift, was frantically working the till, while the manager ran around keeping one eye on him. I gulped down my sandwich, ready to change into my uniform and rush out to help at any moment.

For breakfast I eat convenience store bread, for lunch I eat convenience store rice balls with something from the hot-food cabinet, and after work I'm often so tired I just buy something from the store and take it home for dinner. I drink about half the bottle of water while I'm at work, then put it in my ecobag and take it home with me to finish at night. When I think that my body is entirely made up of food from this store, I feel like I'm as much a part of the store as the magazine racks or the coffee machine.

After breakfast, I check the weather forecast and go over the store's data. The weather forecast is a vital source of information for a convenience store. The difference in temperature from the previous day is an important factor. Today will have a high of 21°C and low of 14°C. It will be cloudy, with rain forecast in the evening, when it will feel cooler.

On hot days sandwiches sell briskly, whereas on cold days rice balls, meat dumplings, and buns are more popular. The sale of food from the counter cabinets also varies according to the temperature. In our branch, croquettes sell well on cold days. Today there also happened to be a sales promotion running on them, so we should make a lot of them, I noted to myself.

The other day-shift staff always start arriving about now, just after eight thirty, when the door opens and a husky voice calls out: "Morning!" It is Mrs. Izumi, our trusty supervisor. She's a housewife, one year older than me at age thirty-seven, and rather stern, but she's an efficient worker. She's a rather flashy dresser and changes out of her high heels into sneakers by her locker.

"Early again today, Miss Furukura? Oh, that's one of those new buns, isn't it? What's it like?" she asked, her eyes settling on the mango-chocolate bun in my hand.

"The cream tastes weird, and it smells a bit strong, which is quite off-putting. It's not very nice, actually."

"Really? Oh dear, the manager ordered a hundred of them. Well, let's at least try to sell the ones that arrived today."

"Hai!"

By far most of the store workers are university students or job-hoppers, and it's unusual for me to work with a woman my age.

Mrs. Izumi tied her hair back and put on a white shirt and light blue tie over her navy-blue jersey blouse. When the current owner took over, he made us all start wearing a shirt and tie under our uniforms, although it was never the rule before. She was checking her appearance in the mirror when Sugawara came flying in calling out: "Good morning!"

Sugawara is twenty-four, a loud and cheerful type. She's a singer in a band and goes on about wanting to dye her short hair red. She's a bit plump and not without a certain charm, but often used to be late and was frequently scolded by the manager for wearing earrings at work. Thanks to Mrs. Izumi's forthright manner of scolding and educating her, however, she now takes her job much more seriously and is an enthusiastic member of staff.

Also on the day shift are Iwaki, a tall and lanky university student, and job-hopper Yukishita, who's now found a proper job and will be leaving soon. Iwaki has also said he'll be looking for a job and will have to take more days off, so the manager thinks he'll either have to come back to the day shift or employ someone new if the store is to keep running smoothly.

My present self is formed almost completely of the people around me. I am currently made up of 30 percent Mrs. Izumi, 30 percent Sugawara, 20 percent the manager, and the rest absorbed from past colleagues such as Sasaki, who left six months ago, and Okasaki, who was our supervisor until a year ago.

My speech is especially infected by everyone around me and is currently a mix of that of Mrs. Izumi and Sugawara. I think the same goes for most people. When some of Sugawara's band members came into the store recently they all dressed and spoke just like her. After Mrs. Izumi came, Sasaki started sounding just like her when she said, "Good job, see you tomorrow!" Once a woman who had gotten on well with Mrs. Izumi at her previous store came to help out, and she dressed so much like Mrs. Izumi I almost mistook the two. And I probably infect others with the way I speak too. Infecting each other like this is how we maintain ourselves as human is what I think.

Outside work Mrs. Izumi is rather flashy, but she dresses the way normal women in their thirties do, so I take cues from the brand of shoes she wears and the label of the coats in her locker. Once she left her makeup bag lying around in the back room and I took a peek inside and made a note of the cosmetics she uses. People would notice if I copied her exactly, though, so what I do is read blogs by people who wear the same clothes she does and go for the other brands of clothes and kinds of shawls they talk about buying. Mrs. Izumi's clothes, accessories, and hairstyles always strike me as the model of what a woman in her thirties should be wearing.

As we were chatting in the back room, her gaze suddenly fell on the ballet flats I was wearing. "Oh, those shoes are from that shop in Omotesando, aren't they? I like that place too. I have some boots from there." In the back room she speaks in a languid drawl, the end of her words slightly drawn out. I bought these flats after checking the brand name of the shoes she wears for work while she was in the toilet.

"Oh really? Wait, do you mean those dark blue ones you wore to the shop before? Those were cute!" I answered, copying Sugawara's speech pattern, but using a slightly more adult tone. Her speech is a rather excitable staccato, the exact opposite of Mrs. Izumi's, but mixing the two styles works surprisingly well.

"We've got quite similar tastes, haven't we? I like your bag too," Mrs. Izumi said with a smile.

It's only natural that my tastes would match hers since I'm copying her. I'm sure everyone must see me as someone with an age-appropriate bag and a manner of speech that has a perfect sense of distance without being reserved or rude.

"Mrs. Izumi, were you in yesterday?" Sugawara called out loudly as she changed by the lockers. "The stock of ramen noodles is in a total mess!"

"Yes, I was here. It was all right in the afternoon, but that kid on the night shift didn't turn up again so it must have been the new guy, Dat-kun."

Pulling up the zip on her uniform as she came over to us, Sugawara pulled a face. "What, he left us in the lurch again? I can't believe it! He knows how short-staffed we are right now. No wonder the store's falling apart. There aren't any drink cartons out there at all and it's the morning rush!"

"I know. It's awful, isn't it? The manager says he'll have to stick to the night shift. He's only got new people on it at the moment."

"We're already having to manage without Iwaki on the day shift since he's taking so much time off for job interviews. What are we going to do? If people want to leave that's fine, but they should make sure they give enough notice. Otherwise they're just making things difficult for the rest of us."

Hearing the two of them speak with such feeling, I felt a twinge of anxiety. There wasn't a trace of anger in my body. I stole a glance at Sugawara and tried to mimic the way she moved her facial muscles as she spoke, the same way I did in training, and parroted, "Really, he left us in the lurch again? I can't believe he'd do that knowing how short-staffed we are."

Mrs. Izumi laughed as she removed her watch and rings.

"Ha ha ha! You're really worked up about it, aren't you Miss Furukura? But you're right. It's really not okay."

I'd noticed soon after starting the job that whenever I got angry at the same things as everyone else, they all seemed happy. If I went along with the manager when he was annoyed or joined in the general irritation at someone skiving off the night shift, there was a strange sense of solidarity as everyone seemed pleased that I was angry too.

Now, too, I felt reassured by the expression on Mrs. Izumi and Sugawara's faces: Good, I pulled off being a "person." I'd felt similarly reassured any number of times here in the convenience store.

Mrs. Izumi looked at the clock and announced, "Well then, time for our morning practice session."

"Okay."

The three of us stood in a row and started our morning routine. Mrs. Izumi opened the report book and informed us of the day's goals and matters to be attended to.

"Today's special is the mango-chocolate bun. Let's all remember to keep announcing it. Also, it's cleanliness crackdown time. Lunchtime is busy, but even so let's be diligent about keeping the floor, windows, and the area around the door clean. We're running out of time, so I'll just trust you to get on with it. Well then, let's practice our phrases, shall we? All together, repeat after me: *Irasshaimasé!*"

"Irasshaimasé!"

"*Certainly. Right away, sir!*"

"Certainly. Right away, sir!"

"*Thank you for your custom!*"

"Thank you for your custom!"

We three repeated in unison the phrases we used with customers, checked our appearance, and one by one filed into the store calling out "Irasshaimasé!" as we went. I was the last to rush through the office door.

"Irasshaimasé! Good morning!"

I love this moment. It feels like "morning" itself is being loaded into me. The tinkle of the door chime as a customer comes in sounds like church bells to my ears. When I open the door, the brightly lit box awaits me—a dependable, normal world that keeps turning. I have faith in the world inside the light-filled box.

* * *

My days off are Friday and Sunday, and on Fridays I sometimes go to see a friend who is now married and lives in the area we grew up in.

At school I'd been so intent on not speaking that I didn't make any friends, but later on after I'd already started working, I got to know her after going to an alumni reunion.

"Wow, Furukura, you look totally different!" Miho had told me cheerfully at that reunion, then went on to comment excitedly how we both had the same bag in different colors. "We should really go shopping together sometime." And so we exchanged e-mail addresses and from time to time meet up for lunch or to go shopping.

After Miho married, she and her husband bought a secondhand house where she now often holds little parties with her friends. There are times when I feel like it's too much bother, knowing I have to work the next day. But it's the only connection I have to the world outside the convenience store and a precious opportunity to mingle with "normal" women my age, so I usually accept her invitations. Today there was Yukari and her young child, and Satsuki, who was married but still childless, and we had all brought cakes along to have with tea.

Yukari had been away with her husband on a job placement, so it was the first time we'd seen her for quite some while. We all laughed as she kept looking around, saying how much she'd missed us as we nibbled at the cakes from the station mall.

"There's really nowhere like home. The last time we met was just after I got married, wasn't it, Keiko?"

"Yes! It was at that celebration barbecue, wasn't it? There were lots of us there that time. Oh, what fun that was!" I said excitedly, mixing Mrs. Izumi and Sugawara's speech patterns.

"You've changed somehow." She stared at me. "Didn't you use to speak more normally? Maybe it's just your hairstyle, but somehow there's a different air about you."

"You think?" Miho asked, tilting her head questioningly. "I don't feel she's changed at all, although it could just be because we meet so often."

But Yukari was right I thought. After all, I absorb the world around me, and that's changing all the time. Just as all the water that was in my body last time we met has now been replaced with new water, the things that make up me have changed too. When we last met a few years ago, most of the store workers were laid-back university students, so of course my way of speaking was different then.

"I guess. Yes, I have probably changed," I said with a smile, not elaborating.

"Come to think of it, your fashion sense has changed too. I'm sure you never used to dress so flash-ily," Satsuki said.

"Oh! Yes, maybe you're right," Miho agreed. "That skirt is from a boutique in Omotesando, isn't it? I tried on the same one in a different color. It's really cute!"

"Isn't it? Lately all the clothes I wear come from that place."

It was the me with different clothes and speech rhythms that was smiling. Who was it that my friends were talking to? Yet Yukari was still smiling at me, repeating again how much she'd missed me.

Miho and Satsuki wear exactly the same expression and speak the same way, perhaps because they live close to each other and often meet up. The way they eat cookies is especially similar, both breaking off tiny pieces and putting them in their mouths with hands that have perfectly manicured nails. I couldn't help wondering whether they had always been like that, but my memory was hazy. The little habits and gestures they had last time I met them must have already been flushed out of my mind I thought to myself.

"Next time let's get more of us together. Especially now that Yukari's back home. Like Shiho, for one."

"Mm, yes. Great idea. Let's do that!"

At Miho's suggestion, we all leaned forward.

"Everyone should bring their husbands and kids too. Let's do another barbecue!"

"Yay! That's a fab idea. It'd be great if all our kids can make friends with each other."

"Yeah, good thinking!"

Satsuki sounded a bit envious, so Yukari prompted her. "You are planning on having kids, aren't you, Satsuki?"

"Sure, I want them. I've been relying on nature to take its course, but I suppose I should start being a bit more proactive about conceiving."

"Oh yes," Miho said. "The timing is perfect now."

I noticed Satsuki gazing at Miho's sleeping baby and got the impression that both of their wombs were resonating in sync.

Yukari had been nodding during their exchange, but now she abruptly directed her gaze to me. "Keiko, aren't you married yet?"

"No, I'm not."

"Really? But . . . you're not still stuck in the same job, are you?"

I thought a moment. I knew it was considered weird for someone of my age to not have either a proper job or be married because my sister had explained it to me. Even so, I balked at being evasive in front of Miho and the others, who knew the truth.

"Yep, I'm afraid so."

Yukari looked flustered by my answer and so I hastily added, "I'm not very strong, so I'm better off in a casual job."

I've made it known among old friends that I have certain health issues that make it more convenient for me to have a part-time job. At my workplace, I tell them it's because my parents are ill and I need to care for them. I have my sister to thank for thinking up these excuses for me.

When I was in my early twenties it wasn't unusual to be a freeter, so I didn't really need to make excuses.

But subsequently everyone started hooking up with society, either through employment or marriage, and I was the only one who hadn't done either.

While I always say it's because I'm frail, deep down everyone must be thinking that if that's so, why would I choose to do a job in which I'm on my feet for long periods every day?

"Do you mind if I ask you a personal question? Have you ever been in love, Keiko?" Satsuki asked teasingly.

"In love?"

"Like, have you ever dated anyone? Come to think of it, I've never heard you talk about that sort of thing."

"Oh I see. No, I haven't," I answered automatically.

Everyone fell quiet and exchanged uncomfortable glances with each other. Too late I remembered that my sister had told me in such cases I should give a vague answer like: "Well, there was someone I liked but I'm not a good judge of men." This would give the impression that I'd at least had a lover or something that might have involved some kind of physical relationship, even if I'd never had an actual boyfriend. "You can just give a vague answer to a personal question, and they'll come to their own conclusions," she'd told me. Well, I messed that one up, I thought to myself.

"You know, I've got quite a few gay friends," Miho intervened, "So I kind of get it. These days you can also be asexual or whatever you like."

"Oh yes, I heard that's on the increase. Like there are young people who just aren't interested in it at all."

"I saw a program on TV about that. It's apparently really hard for them to come out too."

I'd never experienced sex, and I'd never even had any particular awareness of my own sexuality. I was indifferent to the whole thing and had never really given it any thought. And here was everyone taking it for granted that I must be miserable when I wasn't. Even if I had been, though, it didn't follow that my anguish would be the obvious type of anguish they were all talking about. But they didn't want to think it through that far. I had the feeling I was being told they wanted to settle the matter this way because that was the easiest option for them.

It was the same as when I'd hit that boy with a shovel at school. All the adults had jumped to the unfounded conclusion that I must be an abused child and blamed my family. That way they could understand why I'd done such a terrible thing and therefore have peace of mind. So they'd all pressed me to admit my family situation was to blame for what I'd done.

What a pain I thought, wondering why everyone felt such a need for reassurance. But out loud I just parroted the excuse my sister had told me to use whenever I was in a fix: "No, no. It's just because I'm not strong. That's all!"

"Oh yes, it's true, you've got a chronic condition, haven't you? It must be really tough on you."

"You've been like that for ages now. Are you okay?"

I wished I was back in the convenience store where I was valued as a working member of staff and things weren't as complicated as this. Once we donned our uniforms, we were all equals regardless of gender, age, or nationality—all simply store workers.

I looked at the clock—3:00 p.m.—so they'd have finished settling the cash register account and changing money at the bank and would be starting to put the latest truckload of bread and lunch boxes out on display.

Even when I'm far away, the convenience store and I are connected. In my mind's eye I picture the brightly lit and bustling store, and I silently stroke my right hand, its nails neatly trimmed in order to better work the buttons on the cash register.

*   *   *

Whenever I wake up early, I make a point of getting off the train one station before my stop and walking the rest of the way to the store. As I walk, the surrounding apartments and restaurants gradually give way to office blocks.

The sensation that the world is slowly dying feels good. The view is unchanged since that day I first happened on the store. Early in the morning there are no living creatures in sight other than the occasional suit-clad salaryman rushing past.

There are only offices here, but still some of the customers who come into the convenience store look like ordinary residents, and I always wonder where on earth they live. I absently imagine them asleep somewhere within this cast-off-cicada-shell world.

When night falls, the brightly lit office windows transform the area into a geometrically aligned landscape. Unlike the lively area in which my cheap apartment is located, the light is cold and lifeless, all one uniform color.

For a convenience store worker, walking through the area around the store is a way to glean valuable information. If a nearby restaurant starts selling lunch boxes it will impact our sales, and road works starting up will mean more customers. It was really tough when a rival closed down four years after our store opened and we were inundated with their customers. We all had to work overtime since the lunchtime peak had gone on and on, and when we ran out of lunch boxes the manager was reprimanded by head office for not doing enough research. That's when I decided to walk around the area keeping my eye on things to make sure nothing like that ever happened again.

Today there wasn't any major change, other than it looked like a new building was nearing completion, which would probably mean more customers when it opened. I made a mental note of this, then made my way to the store. There I bought a sandwich and some tea and went into the back room to find the store manager, who had been on the night shift again, his sweaty body huddled over the store computer inputting figures.

"Good morning!"

"Oh, morning Miss Furukura. Early again today, I see!"

The store manager is thirty years old and always businesslike. He's manager #8. He has a sharp tongue but works hard.

Manager #2 was always slacking off, while #4 was dependable and liked cleaning, and #6, who was rather eccentric and generally disliked, had caused a scandal when the entire night shift walked out on him en masse. Manager #8 is comparatively popular with part-timers and is the type who engages in physical tasks, so I like watching him at work. Manager #7 was a wimp and wasn't strict enough with the night shift, so the store ended up a mess. While #8 might be a bit brusque, I thought looking at him, in this respect he was easier to work with.

For eighteen years, there has always been a manager, even if his appearance keeps changing. Although each is different, taken all together I sometimes have the feeling they are but one single creature.

Manager #8 has a loud voice, and it booms around the back room.

"Oh, today you'll be on with that new guy, Shiraha," he told me. "He did his training at night, so it'll be his first time on the day shift. Look after him, will you?"

"Yes, I will!" I answered energetically, and the manager nodded several times as he continued to input figures without pause.

"You know, Miss Furukura, I can always rest easy when you're here. Iwaki has gone for good now, so it'll just be you, Mrs. Izumi, Sugawara, and now Shiraha on the frontline day shift. It looks like I'm going to have to stay on the night shift for the time being, so I'm relying on you."

The manager has a way of drawing out the ends of his words just like Mrs. Izumi does, although their tones of voice are completely different. He came after Mrs. Izumi, so it was probably she who infected him, while she in turn probably absorbed his way of talking and ended up lengthening her drawl.

Thinking about this I nodded and, imitating Sugawara's speech, said, "Sure, no problem! The sooner we get someone new the better!"

"Yeah, I've put up help wanted ads, and I've also asked the guys on the night shift if they have any friends looking for a job. Your being able to come in five days a week on the day shift is a big help, Miss Furukura."

In a short-staffed convenience store, a store worker can sometimes be highly appreciated just by existing, by virtue of not rocking the boat. I'm not particularly brilliant compared to Mrs. Izumi and Sugawara, but I'm second to none in terms of never being late or taking days off. I just come in every day without fail, and because of that I'm accepted as a well-functioning part of the store.

Just then a thin voice came from the other side of the door.

"Um . . ."

"Oh, Shiraha, it's you. Come in, come in!" the manager said. "Didn't I tell you to arrive thirty minutes early? You're late!"

The door opened quietly, and a tall man, almost six feet and lanky like a wire coat hanger, came in, his head drooping.

He looked as though he were made of wire, and his glasses were like silver twined around his face. He was wearing a white shirt and black trousers as dictated by the store rules, but he was too skinny and the shirt didn't fit him, so that while his wrists were exposed, the fabric was unnaturally puckered around his stomach.

I covered my shock at his skin-and-bone appearance by quickly lowering my head in greeting.

"Pleased to meet you! I'm Furukura, from the day shift. Looking forward to working with you!"

The way I said this was probably close to the store manager's speech. Shiraha flinched at my loud voice and answered noncommittally: "Um, ah . . ."

"Come on, Shiraha! Where are your manners?" the manager admonished him. "It's essential to get off to a good start, so make your greetings properly."

"Um, ah . . . good morning," Shiraha mumbled, barely audible.

"As from today you've finished your training and are now a fully fledged member of the day shift, you know. You've been taught how to work the cash register and do the cleaning and how to make basic counter foods, but there's still a lot to learn. This is Miss Furukura, who's been working here ever since the store opened, can you believe? Ask her if there's anything you need to know."

"Um, ah . . ."

"She's been here eighteen years, you know. Eighteen years! I bet that surprised you, didn't it, Shiraha? You have to look up to her, you know."

"What?" Shiraha said, a dubious expression on his face. His sunken eyes seemed to retreat even farther into his head.

I was just wondering how I could dispel the awkward atmosphere when the door flew open and Sugawara appeared.

"Mornin' all!" she called out cheerfully as she came in, a bass guitar case slung across her back. Noticing Shiraha, she added, "Oh, a newcomer! Nice to meet you. So glad you're here."

It seemed to me that Sugawara's voice had gotten even louder since manager #8 took over. I was just thinking how that was a bit creepy when I noticed that Sugawara and Shiraha were ready to start.

"Well then, I'll lead the morning session today, shall I?" the manager said. "First, today's particulars. Shiraha here has completed his training and will be working nine to five starting today. Make sure your voice is loud enough when you greet customers, won't you, Shiraha?

Anything you don't know you can ask from these two here. They're both veterans. And if possible, take over the till during the lunchtime rush, will you?"

"Oh, er, okay," Shiraha nodded.

"Next, frankfurters are on promotion today, so make sure you prepare enough of them. We're aiming to sell a hundred! Last time we sold eighty-three, so we can do it. We really can! Keep them coming, all right? I'm depending on you, Miss Furukura."

"Hai!" I answered brightly at the top of my lungs.

"The weather is important to the store too, you know. It's warmed up quite a lot, so cold things will sell well today. Be sure to check the drink stocks in the refrigerators and restock them when necessary. Also, the shout-out to customers today is the frankfurters promotion and the new mango custard dessert."

"Okay!" Sugawara responded at once.

"Well, those are the main points for today. Now let's go over our pledge and the six most important phrases for dealing with customers. Repeat after me!"

Following the manager's cue, we repeated the phrases at the top of our lungs.

"We pledge to provide our customers with the best service and to aim to make our store the beloved store of choice in the area."

"We pledge to provide our customers with the best service and to aim to make our store the beloved store of choice in the area."

"Irasshaimasé!"

"Irasshaimasé!"

"Yes, madam. Right away, madam."

"Yes, madam. Right away, madam."

"Thank you very much!"

"Thank you very much!"

The three of us raised our voices in unison following the prompts. I was just thinking how much brisker the morning session was when the manager led it, when Shiraha muttered under his breath: "Ugh, it's just like a religion!"

Of course it is, I thought.

From now on, we existed only in the service of the convenience store. It appeared Shiraha had not yet come to terms with this, for he only moved his mouth mechanically, hardly making his voice audible.

"That's the end of the morning session. Let's all do our best again today!"

"We will!" Sugawara and I responded.

"Well then, if there's anything you don't understand, don't hesitate to ask," I said to Shiraha. "I'm depending on you!"

Shiraha snickered. "Huh. Anything I don't understand? About a part-time job in a convenience store?"

He gave a loud snort of laughter, and I watched as a bubble of snot formed in his nostril. So there's enough moisture behind Shiraha's papery dry skin for mucus to form, I thought, distracted by the sight of it bursting.

"Not particularly. I pretty much get it."

"Oh, have you worked in a store before?" Sugawara asked.

"What? No, I haven't," he muttered.

"Well in that case, you still have a lot to learn!" the manager told him. "Start by checking the product displays, will you Miss Furukura? I'm off home to get some sleep now."

"Will do!"

"I'll take the till!" Sugawara said and rushed off.

I took Shiraha over to the drink cartons and, using Sugawara's style of speech, said: "Well, let's get started, then! Drink cartons sell particularly well in the morning, so make sure the display's nice and neat. And check that the price cards are in place, okay? And don't forget shout-outs and customer greetings while you work. And make sure you get out of the way quickly if a customer wants to buy something."

"Yeah, all right," Shiraha said and half-heartedly started straightening the drink cartons.

"Let me know once you've finished that, and I'll show you how to do the cleaning."

He carried on working without bothering to answer.

I went to help out on the till for the morning rush. By the time the lines had subsided and I went back to check on Shiraha, he was nowhere in sight. The drinks cabinet was a mess, with milk cartons placed among the orange juice.

I went in search of him, only to find him idly flicking through the store manual.

"What's the matter? Is there something you don't understand?"

Turning over another page, he answered pomp-ously: "You know, for a chain store manual this isn't very good. Kind of misses the mark I'd say. You have to start by doing this sort of thing properly, otherwise the company will never improve. That's what I think."

"Shiraha, you haven't finished tidying the displays like I asked you to, have you?"

"Uh, yeah, I did," he said without looking up from the manual.

I went up to him and raised my voice. "Shiraha, the store displays are more important than the manual! Keeping them neat, along with the customer greetings and shout-outs, are the two most basic of the basic tasks of a store worker, you know! If you don't understand how, let's do it together."

Ignoring his irritation, I took him back to the drink cartons and rearranged the display while talking him through it in simple terms. "Line things up neatly so they're facing the customer, like this! And don't mess up the order of the products. Vegetable juice goes here and soy milk here."

"This sort of work isn't suited to men," he mut-tered. "After all, things haven't changed since the Stone

Age, have they? Men go hunting and women keep the home and gather fruit and wild herbs while they wait for the men to come back. This type of work is more suited to the way women's brains are set up."

"Shiraha, we're in the twenty-first century! Here in the convenience store we're not men and women. We're all store workers. Oh, there's some stock in the back room. Let's go and sort that out together so you can see how it's done."

I took some of the stock out of the walk-in refrigerator, explained to Shiraha how to refill the displays, and then hurried back to my own work.

As I carried some boxes of frankfurters over to the cash register, I noticed Sugawara frowning as she filled the coffee machine with beans.

"That guy is weird, isn't he? He's only just finished his training and today's his first day, right? He hasn't even spent any time on the till yet, and here he is telling me to let him place the orders!"

"Really?"

Well, at least he was keen to do something, which wasn't necessarily a bad thing I thought. She looked up at me and smiled, dimples forming in her plump cheeks.

"Nothing ever fazes you, does it, Miss Furukura?"

"What?"

"No, really, you're amazing. I can't stand that sort of guy. He just rubs me the wrong way. But you, well, sometimes you join in when me and Mrs. Izumi are wound up about something, but you yourself never complain, do you? I've never seen you get upset even with an annoying newbie."

I was startled. I had the feeling I was being told I was a fake and hastily rearranged my expression.

"That's not true! It's just that I don't let it show."

"Wow, really?" She giggled. "I'd be really shocked if you lost your temper with me, Miss Furukura."

She was now calm, while I had to pay the utmost attention to the way I moved my facial muscles and formed my words.

I heard the sound of a basket being put down by the cash register and quickly turned to see a regular customer standing there leaning on her walking stick.

"Irasshaimasé!" I called out and started briskly scanning the product bar codes.

The woman narrowed her eyes and said, "This place never changes, does it?"

I paused, then answered, "You're right, it doesn't!"

Nevertheless, the store manager, the store assistants, the disposable chopsticks, the spoons, the uniforms, the milk and eggs I'd just run through the bar code scanner, the plastic bag I placed them in—none of these had been in the store right from the very beginning. The same items had always been in their places, but they were continually being replaced. Maybe it made sense to say the store never changes.

As I thought about this, I informed the customer at the top of my lungs: "That'll be three hundred and ninety yen please!"

*   *   *

On Friday, my day off, I headed to the residential district in Yokohama where my sister lived in a condo in a new housing development opposite the station. Her husband commuted to his job at an electric company and almost always came home on the last train.

The apartment wasn't all that large, but it was new and smart and comfortably furnished.

"Hey, come on in! I've just put Yutaro to sleep."

"Thanks," I said and tiptoed inside. It was the first time I'd visited my sister since my nephew was born.

"So how is it being a parent? It must be hard work!"

"Well yeah, but I'm getting used to it. It's much better now that he sleeps at night."

When I first saw my nephew through the glass window at the hospital, he looked like an alien creature. But now he'd grown into something more humanlike, complete with hair.

We sat down to eat the cake I'd brought, accompanied by normal tea for me and caffeine-free rooibos tea for Mami.

"Delicious. I hardly ever get out now Yutaro is here, so I don't get to eat anything like this."

"Glad you like it."

"Whenever you give me food, it reminds me of when we were little," she said with an embarrassed smile.

I stroked my sleeping nephew's cheek with my forefinger. It felt strangely soft, like stroking a blister.

"You know, when I look at Yutaro, I think, 'Yeah, he really is just an animal,'" my sister said happily. The boy was frail and often came down with a fever, so she was always fussing over him. She couldn't help feeling anxious, despite knowing fevers were common for babies and he would be okay.

"So how are you? Work going well?"

"Sure, I'm doing fine. Oh, and I went to see Miho and the others back home recently."

"What, again? Lucky them! You should come and see your nephew more often," she said, laughing.

As far as I was concerned, though, there wasn't any difference between Miho's child and my nephew, and I didn't understand the logic of coming out all the way here just to see him. Maybe this particular baby should be more important to me than the others. But so far as I could see, aside from a few minor differences they were all just an animal called a baby and looked much the same, just like stray cats all looked much the same.

"Oh, come to think of it, Mami, I wanted to ask you if you can come up with a better excuse for me. Lately when I tell them I'm not very strong, they give me disbelieving looks."

"Okay, I'll have a think about it. But anyway, you're being rehabilitated, so it's not like you're lying exactly. No need to be embarrassed about it."

"But once they get it into their heads that I'm not normal, since they all think they are normal they'll give me a hard time about it, won't they? That'd be a lot of bother. So it'd be handy to have an excuse to fend them off with."

When something was strange, everyone thought they had the right to come stomping in all over your life to figure out why. I found that arrogant and infuriating, not to mention a pain in the neck. Sometimes I even wanted to hit them with a shovel to shut them up, like I did that time in elementary school.

But I recalled how upset my sister had been when I'd casually mentioned this to her before and kept my mouth shut.

She had always been kind to me ever since we were little, and I never wanted to hurt her, so I changed the subject and said cheerfully, "Oh, that reminds me. I met Yukari for the first time in ages, and she told me I'd changed."

"Yeah, you are a bit different from the way you used to be."

"I am? But then so are you, Mami. I get the impression you're more like a grown-up than before."

"What do you mean by that? I've been an adult for some time now."

My sister now had crow's feet, the way she talked was much more relaxed, and her clothes were monotone. There were probably lots of people like this in her life now I thought.

The baby started to cry. My sister hurriedly picked him up and tried to soothe him. What a lot of hassle I thought. I looked at the small knife we'd used to cut the cake still lying there on the table: if it was just a matter of making him quiet, it would be easy enough. My sister cuddled him tightly to her. Watching them, I wiped some cream from the cake off my lip.

*   *   *

The following morning when I arrived at work, the store was shrouded in an unusually tense atmosphere. Entering through the automatic door, I saw a regular customer looking fearfully over at the magazine corner. A woman who always came to buy coffee rushed past me and out of the store, and two men were standing by the bakery section talking under their breath.

Wondering what on earth was going on, I glanced in the direction the customers were looking and realized they were all eyeing a middle-aged man in a shabby suit.

He was walking around the store, talking to various customers. I strained my ears to hear what he was saying, and he appeared to be telling them off. "Hey, you there. Stop making the floor dirty!" he said shrilly to a man with dirty shoes and then to a woman perusing the chocolates: "Oy! Stop messing up the display!" Everyone was watching him nervously, afraid he might pick on them next.

A long, straggly line had formed at the cash register, where Dat-kun was frantically working the till while the manager dealt with a parcel delivery order for a set of golf clubs. The man went over to them and roared, "Line up properly along the wall, will you? And make it snappy!" The office workers looked alarmed, but they just wanted to finish their shopping quickly and get back to work, so they avoided eye contact and did their best to ignore him.

I hurried into the back room and took my uniform out of my locker. Watching the security camera as I changed, I saw the male customer head for the magazine corner where he loudly admonished another customer who was standing there reading: "No reading magazines in the store! Come on, buy it or get out!"

The young man who had been shouted at glared at him irritably and called out to Dat-kun, who was furiously working the till. "Hey, who is this guy? From head office?"

Flustered, Dat-kun looked up from the till. "No, he's . . . um . . . a customer."

"What the crap? You don't even work here! Who the hell do you think you are?" the young man demanded, pushing up against the bossy customer. "What gives you the right to go around poking your nose in where it's not wanted?"

Whenever there was any trouble, we were supposed to leave it to a senior employee to deal with. As per the rules, I quickly finished putting on my uniform and ran to the cash register to take over from the manager. "Thanks, that's a great help," he said quietly, then rushed around the counter and slipped himself between the two men. I handed the golf club delivery slip to the customer, keeping an eye on the situation in case it developed into a fight. If that happened, the procedure was to immediately press the alarm.

In the end, the manager apparently handled the situation well and the troublemaker left the store muttering under his breath.

A wave of relief passed through the store, and the morning atmosphere returned to normal.

A convenience store is a forcibly normalized environment where foreign matter is immediately eliminated. The threatening atmosphere that had briefly permeated the store was swept away, and the customers again concentrated on buying their coffee and pastries as if nothing had happened.

"Thank you, Miss Furukura, that was a big help," the manager said once the line at last came to an end and I went to the back room.

"Not at all. I'm glad there wasn't a fight."

"I wonder what on earth got into that guy? I've never seen him before."

Mrs. Izumi was already there in the back room and asked the manager, "Did something happen?"

"No, just a really weird customer was going around the store shouting at people. Luckily he left before causing any real trouble."

"Really? Was he a regular?"

"No, never seen him before. No idea what he was trying to do. He didn't seem like a thug, though. Anyway, if he comes back be sure to contact me right away. We don't want him causing trouble for the other customers."

"Yes, will do."

"Well then, I'll be off home now. I'm on again tonight."

"You must be exhausted. Oh, by the way, can you give Shiraha a talking-to for me? He's always shirking his duties, and he doesn't take any notice of what I tell him."

Mrs. Izumi almost had the status of a head office employee, so she could discuss employee matters like this with the manager.

"He really does seem useless. I've had a bad feeling about him ever since the interview. The way he talks the job down, saying it's *only* a convenience store, like he's taking the piss. So why did he apply in the first place? I only took him on because we're so short-staffed, but . . . he just doesn't listen unless you really spell everything out for him."

"He's often late too. Today he's supposed to be on from nine, but he's not even here yet," Mrs. Izumi said with a frown. "How old is he? Thirty-five or so? And taking a job like this! He's beyond hope, isn't he?"

"A dead-ender. The worst type, just a burden on society. People have a duty to fulfill their role in society either through the workplace or the family."

Mrs. Izumi nodded vigorously, then nudged the manager. "But then sometimes there are special circumstances, like in Miss Furukura's case, which is understandable."

"Ah, yes, right. In Miss Furukura's case it can't be helped. It's different for men and women too!" the manager also hastily added. Before I could respond he went on: "Shiraha's such a loser, though. I've even caught him fiddling with his cell phone while working the till."

"Yes! I've seen him do that too."

"What? While he's working?" I asked in surprise.

It was a fundamental rule never to carry your phone around while at work. I couldn't understand why he'd violate such a simple directive.

"You know I always check the security camera for the times I'm not here, right? Shiraha's new on the job, so I keep an eye on him to see what he's like. On the surface he seems to be doing kind of okay, but he does have a habit of neglecting the work, doesn't he?"

"I'm sorry I never noticed it."

"No, no, it's nothing for you to apologize about, Miss Furukura. You've been doing really well with greeting customers, I must say. Every time I check the camera, I'm impressed. You're really great. You never take time off, and you never do anything less than an excellent job."

Manager #8 was looking over me when he wasn't there and knew that I was a faithful disciple to the store.

"Thank you!" I said, bowing deeply.

Just then the door opened and Shiraha came in.

"Oh . . . good morning," he said listlessly, his voice barely audible. He was all skin and bones and probably needed the suspenders visible through his white shirt to hold his trousers up. The skin on his arms looked as though it was stuck straight onto his bones, and I wondered how all his internal organs could fit into such a skinny body.

"Shiraha, you're late! You should be here changed and ready to start the morning session five minutes before time! And make sure you greet everyone properly with a bright and cheerful 'good morning' when you come into the office. Plus, it's forbidden to use your cell phone except during your breaks. You have it with you when you're working on the till, don't you? I've seen you look at it."

"Ah . . . Oh, sorry . . ." Shiraha was visibly disconcerted. "Um, you mean yesterday? Were you watching me, Miss Furukura?"

He seemed to think I'd told on him. "No," I said, shaking my head.

"The camera, Shiraha," the manager said. "The security camera! When I'm on night shift I always check up on what's been going on during the day shift. Well, maybe I didn't explain the rule against using your cell phone clearly enough, but don't do it, okay?"

"Oh, okay. I didn't know. Sorry."

"Right. Don't do it again. Oh, Mrs. Izumi, will you come out into the store with me? I want to get the summer gifts section up on the aisle end shelves. I want to make a big display this time."

"Sure. The samples have already arrived, haven't they? I'll give you a hand!"

"I want to get it done today. I need to include an extra shelf at the bottom for miscellaneous summer goods, so we have to change the heights of all the shelves. Miss Furukura and Shiraha, can you get on with the morning practice on your own? I want to get this seen to first."

"Yes, we will!"

Once the manager and Mrs. Izumi had left the back room, Shiraha tutted. When I glanced over at him, he spat, "Huh. He sure does talk big for a lowly convenience store manager."

When you work in a convenience store, people often look down on you for working there. I find this fascinating, and I like to look them in the face when they do this to me. And as I do so I always think: that's what a human is.

And sometimes even those who are doing the same job are biased against it. Before I knew what I was doing, I looked Shiraha in the face.

I find the shape of people's eyes particularly interesting when they're being condescending. I see a wariness or a fear of being contradicted or sometimes a belligerent spark ready to jump on any attack. And if they're unaware of being condescending, their glazed-over eyeballs are steeped in a fluid mix of ecstasy and a sense of superiority.

I looked into Shiraha's eyes. There I saw only prejudice in its simplest form.

As if sensing my gaze on him, he opened his mouth to speak, revealing the yellowing roots of teeth that were black in places. He obviously hadn't been to the dentist for a long time.

"Who is he to throw his weight around anyway?" he went on. "He's only employed to run a small store like this, so he's basically a loser, isn't he? Just a useless piece of shit."

They were harsh words, but he muttered them so quietly I somehow didn't get the feeling he really was all that angry. From where I stood, there were two types of prejudiced people—those who had a deep-rooted urge for prejudice and those who unthinkingly repeated a barrage of slurs they'd heard somewhere. Shiraha appeared to be the latter.

He carried on muttering at speed, now and then fumbling his words.

"Everyone here is a stupid loser. It's the same in any convenience store. You'll only find housewives who can't get by on their husbands' salary, job-hoppers without plans for the future, and the crappiest students who can't get better jobs like being a home tutor. Or foreigners who send money home. All losers."

"I see."

He really was just like me, uttering words that sounded human when really he wasn't saying anything at all. But he sure did seem to like the word "loser." He'd used it several times in no time at all. I recalled how Sugawara had said, "Shiraha gives me the creeps, especially the way he's so adept at spouting excuses when what he really wants is to slack off." I nodded. Then a simple question occurred to me, so I put it to him.

"Why did you come to work here, Shiraha?"

"Marriage hunting," he said, as if it were no big deal.

"What?" I exclaimed in surprise. I'd heard all kinds of reasons: "It's close to home" or "it looks fun." But this was the first time I met anyone who'd come to work in a convenience store in order to find a marriage partner.

"But it's a dead loss." Shiraha said. "There's no one here who'd make a decent wife. The young ones are too flighty, and the others are too old."

"Well, most of the workers are university students, and you don't often get anyone of marriageable age."

"Some of the customers are kind of okay, but most of them are too haughty. This place is surrounded by big companies and the type of women who work for them are too domineering for my taste."

I don't know who he thought he was talking to, but all the while he was staring at a notice on the wall that read: LET'S REACH OUR TARGETS FOR THE SUMMER GIFTS!

"They're all after snaring a guy who works at the same company and won't even look at me. Women have been like that since the Stone Age. The youngest, prettiest girls in the village go to the strongest hunters. They leave strong genes, while the rest of us just have to console ourselves with what's left. Our so-called modern society is just an illusion. We're living a world that has hardly changed since prehistoric times. We might go on about equality of the sexes, but—"

"Shiraha, get changed into your uniform, will you? If we don't do the morning practice now we won't finish in time," I said, interrupting his rant against the customers.

He grudgingly picked up his backpack and went to his locker, still muttering to himself as he shoved his things inside it.

As I watched him, the middle-aged man the manager had thrown out of the store earlier came to mind.

"Um, you do realize you'll be fixed?"

"What?" he asked, as if he hadn't heard right.

"Oh, nothing. Hurry up and change so we can do the morning practice!"

A convenience store is a forcibly normalized environment, so the likes of you are fixed right away I thought as I watched him taking his time getting changed. But I didn't say it out loud.

*   *   *

On Monday morning I arrived at the store to find a big red cross through Shiraha's name on the shift roster. I was thinking he must have suddenly taken time off, when Mrs. Izumi turned up, right on time even though it was supposed to be her day off.

"Good morning! Um, what happened with Shiraha?" I asked the manager as he came off his night shift into the back room.

"Ah, Shiraha . . ." He and Mrs. Izumi exchanged a wry look. "Yesterday we had a little talk and decided to leave him off the work roster," the manager said nonchalantly. I wasn't entirely surprised.

"I was willing to overlook his slacking off and even how he would secretly eat the food put out for disposal, but there was a woman customer, a regular, who'd forgotten her parasol and came back to get it, and he started behaving all stalkerish toward her, copying her phone number from the delivery service slip and trying to find out where she lived. Mrs. Izumi here realized what was going on and I checked the security video right away. So I talked to him and told him to leave."

What an idiot, I thought. Store workers sometimes break little rules, but I'd never heard of anything as ugly as this. It was just lucky it hadn't become a police matter.

"The guy was weird from the start. He got the phone number for a girl working the night shift from the store's contact data and started calling her, and then hung around in the back room so he could suggest going home together. He even tried to chat up Mrs. Izumi, who's married. I wish he'd put that much energy into doing the job! You didn't like him either, did you, Miss Furukura?" he said.

Mrs. Izumi made a face. "He really gave me the creeps. What a pervert. When he didn't have any luck with the store workers, he started trying it on with the customers! Just the pits. We really should have had him arrested."

"Oh, he hadn't gone that far, not yet at least."

"It's criminal, you know. Criminal! With his sort, the sooner you have him arrested the better."

For all they were complaining, though, somehow there was an air of relief in the store. Now that Shiraha was no longer there, it had gone back to being the peaceful place it had been before his arrival. And everyone had become strangely cheerful and chatty, as if refreshed now that the nuisance had gone.

"To tell the truth, he was getting on my nerves. I'd rather we were short-staffed!" said Sugawara with a smile as she arrived for her shift. "He was just the worst, always making excuses, and if you warned him about slacking off he'd start going on about the Stone Age. A nutjob, if you ask me."

"Oh yes, that!" Mrs. Izumi burst out laughing. "That Stone Age stuff was weird. What was he going on about? Completely nonsensical! Please don't employ anyone like that again," she added, turning to the manager.

"Well, it was only because we were so short-staffed—"

"Getting fired from a casual job in a convenience store at his age! Hopeless, really. He'd be doing us all a favor if he dropped dead, seriously."

Everyone laughed. "He really would," I said nodding, thinking that if I ever became a foreign object, I'd no doubt be eliminated in much the same way.

"We'll have to find someone else . . . I'd better put up an ad."

And so one of the cells of the store was again being replaced.

After the morning practice, which was livelier than usual, I was on my way to the cash register when I saw a regular customer, a woman with a walking stick, reaching for something on the bottom shelf, bending down so far it looked as though she would topple over.

"Let me help you! Is this what you were after?" I asked, picking up a pot of strawberry jam.

"Thank you," she said with a smile.

I carried her basket to the till. As she fished out her purse to pay, she again muttered, "This place really doesn't ever change, does it?"

Actually, someone was eliminated from here today, I thought. But I merely told her "thank you" and started scanning her purchases.

Her figure overlapped with that of the old lady who had been the very first customer when the store opened eighteen years ago. She too had come daily, walking with a stick, until one day I realized she wasn't coming anymore. Maybe her health had deteriorated, or maybe she'd moved. We had no way of knowing.

But here I was repeating the same scene of that first day. Since then we had greeted the same morning 6,607 times.

I gently placed the eggs in a plastic bag. The same eggs I sold yesterday, only different. The customer put the same chopsticks into the same plastic bag as yesterday, took the same change, and gave the same morning smile.

*   *   *

Miho texted to let me know she was holding a barbecue party at her house on Sunday. I had just promised to help her with the shopping in the morning when my cell phone rang. It was a call from home.

"Keiko, didn't you say you were going to Miho's place tomorrow? Won't you show your face here afterward? Your father misses you."

"Um, I don't think I can. I have to be in good physical shape for work the next day, so I'd better get home early."

"Really? What a pity . . . You didn't come over for New Year's either. Please do come soon."

"Okay."

We were so short-staffed over New Year's that I'd worked every day of the holiday. The convenience store is open 365 days a year, and many of the staff are unable to come in over the New Year, what with housewives being busy with their families and international students returning to their home countries. I'd wanted to go see my parents, but when I realized what a fix the store was in I'd without hesitation opted to work.

"Well, how are you?" my mother went on. "You spend all day on your feet, Keiko. It must be tiring. Um, how have things been lately? What's new?"

Hearing her pry like this, I got the feeling that somehow she was still hoping for some kind of new development in my life. She was probably a bit tired of how I hadn't progressed at all in eighteen years.

When I told her everything was fine as usual, she sounded both relieved and disappointed at once.

After we hung up, I looked at myself in the mirror. I had aged since the day I'd been reborn as a convenience store worker. That didn't bother me, except that I got tired more easily than before. I sometimes wondered what would become of me if I got too old to work here. Manager #6 had to quit his job when he hurt his back and was unable to work. To ensure that didn't happen to me, I had to keep my body in good shape, for the sake of the store.

The next morning, as promised, I helped Miho with the shopping and preparations for the barbecue.

At noon, Miho's husband, Satsuki's husband, and some friends who lived a little way away came over. It was the first time we'd all been together for ages.

Of the fourteen or fifteen people gathered together, there were only two others apart from me who weren't married. I hadn't thought anything of it since not everyone had come as a couple, but unmarried Miki whispered to me: "We're the only ones here who can't hold our heads up high, aren't we?"

"It's been such a long time since I've seen everyone! When was the last time? That hanami party?"

"Same here. It's my first time back since then too."

"So, what are you guys all up to these days?"

For quite a few of the friends gathered, it was the first time they had been back in the area for some time, so one by one we all gave updates on our situations.

"I'm living in Yokohama now. It's better for work, after all."

"Oh, have you changed jobs?"

"Yes! I'm in a fashion accessories firm now. The atmosphere in my previous job was a bit, well . . . you know."

"I got married and live in Saitama now. I'm still in the same job, though."

"As you can see, I had a baby and am on maternity leave," Yukari said, and then it was my turn.

"I'm working part-time in a convenience store. My health . . ."

I was about to give the usual excuse my sister had made for me, when Eri leaned forward. "Part-time? Oh, so that means you got married!" she said, as if it were self-evident. "When was that?"

"No, I didn't," I answered.

"But, then, how come you're only doing that sort of job?" Mamiko asked, puzzled.

"Well, you see, my health . . ."

"You see, Keiko's not very strong, and that's why she doesn't have a regular job," Miho said, covering for me.

I started to thank Miho for speaking up for me, but Yukari's husband butted in suspiciously. "What? But you have to be on your feet all day in a job like that."

It was the first time I'd ever met him, and here he was leaning forward and frowning at me as if questioning my very existence.

"Um, well, I don't have any experience of other jobs, and the store is comfortable for me both physically and mentally."

He stared at me as though I were some kind of alien. "What, you never . . .? I mean, if finding a job is so hard, then at least you should get married. Look, these days there are always things like online marriage sites, you know," he sputtered.

As I watched, some of his spittle flew out and landed on the barbecue meat. He really should avoid leaning forward over food when talking, I thought. But then Miho's husband started nodding vigorously too.

"That's right, why don't you just find someone? It doesn't really matter who it is, after all. Women have it easy in that sense. It'd be disastrous if you were a man, though."

"How about if we find someone for you? Yoji, you have a wide circle of connections, don't you?" asked Satsuki.

"Yes, great idea!" Miho and the others exclaimed excitedly. "Can you think of anyone? There must be someone just right for her."

Miho's husband whispered in her ear, then forced a smile. "Oh, but all my friends are married now . . . no, it's impossible. There's no one."

"So why don't you register on a marriage site? We should take a photo now for you to use. For that sort of thing, it's best not to use a selfie. You're much more likely to come across as likable and get lots of responses with a photo of you surrounded by a lot of other people, like today's barbecue."

"Yes, it's true! Come on, let's take a photo now!" Miho said.

Stifling a laugh, Yukari's husband said, "Yes, it's a golden opportunity!"

"Opportunity? Do you think any good can come out of it?" I asked naively.

He looked flustered. "Well, worth trying, the sooner the better. You can't go on like this, and deep down you must be getting desperate, no? Once you get past a certain age it'll be too late."

"I can't go on like this? You mean I shouldn't be living the way I am now? Why do you say that?"

I genuinely wanted to know, but I heard Miho's husband mutter in a low voice: "Oh, for crying out loud."

"I'm getting desperate too," Miki chimed in. Then she added breezily: "But I'm always traveling abroad on business."

"Well, you've got a high-flying job, Miki," Yukari's husband said soothingly. "You earn more than most men, which I guess makes it pretty hard to find a good match."

"Oh, the meat's burning. The meat!" Miho shouted, distracting everyone's attention and, relieved, they all began helping themselves to meat. Everyone was biting into the meat that had been sprayed by Yukari's husband's saliva.

The next thing I knew, just like that time in elementary school, they all turned their backs on me and started edging away, staring curiously at me over their shoulders as though contemplating some ghastly life form.

Oh, I thought absently, I've become a foreign object.

In my mind's eye I saw Shiraha, who had been forced to leave the store. Maybe it would be my turn next.

The normal world has no room for exceptions and always quietly eliminates foreign objects. Anyone who is lacking is disposed of.

So *that's* why I need to be cured. Unless I'm cured, normal people will expurgate me.

Finally I understood why my family had tried so hard to fix me.

* * *

Somehow I felt the need to hear the sound of the convenience store, so on my way home from Miho's that evening I dropped into work.

"Hey, Miss Furukura, what's up?" The high school girl on the evening shift was busy doing some cleaning but paused when she caught sight of me. "Wasn't it your day off today?"

"Yes, that's right. I went to visit my parents, but I thought I'd just place a few orders on my way home."

"Wow, amazing, you're really dedicated, aren't you?"

The manager had arrived early and was in the back room.

"Good evening. Are you about to start your shift?" I asked him.

"Oh, Miss Furukura, what brings you in now?"

"I got back earlier than expected, and since I was passing nearby I thought I'd just come and input some figures . . ."

"Oh, you mean the confectionery orders? I dealt with those earlier, but you can check them for me if you like."

"Thank you."

The manager looked a bit pale. Maybe he hadn't been getting enough sleep.

I sat down at the store computer and got to work.

"How are things on the night shift? Do you think you'll have enough people?"

"No, not really. Someone came for an interview, but I didn't take him on. After what happened with Shiraha, I'd better make sure I hire someone we can use next time."

The manager often says "someone we can use," and I wonder whether I'm someone we can use or not. Maybe I'm working because I want to be a useful tool.

"What was he like?"

"Oh, he was fine. But agewise . . . He's already retired and had just left his previous job because of a bad back. And he said he wanted to be able to take time off work here too when his back was bad. It might be all right if I know in advance, but if I'm going to have him take time off at the last minute, I'm probably better off just doing the night shift myself."

"I see."

When you do physical labor, you end up being no longer useful when your physical condition deteriorates. However hard I work, however dependable I am, when my body grows old then no doubt I too will be a worn-out part, ready to be replaced, no longer of any use to the convenience store.

"Oh, Miss Furukura, could you work this Sunday, just the afternoon? Sugawara has a gig and won't be able to come in."

"Yes, I can do that."

"Really? That's such a big help."

For now I was still a usable tool. Feeling a mix of both relief and anxiety, I said, mimicking Sugawara's way of talking, "No, I'm trying to save money, so it suits me just fine," and I smiled.

* * *

I only noticed Shiraha standing outside the store by chance.

It was night, and a plump shadow on a corner in the deserted office district reminded me of a game I had played when I was little. I would stare hard at my shadow on the ground then quickly look up at the sky—and see my own shadow up there. I strained my eyes to see who this shadow on the wall might belong to. As I approached, I realized it was Shiraha, nervously huddled next to a building, trying to keep himself hidden.

He looked as though he was waiting for the woman customer he'd been stalking. I remembered the manager saying how the woman always stopped at the convenience store on her way home from work to buy some dried fruit, so he'd hang around in the back room until that time.

"Shiraha, next time they'll call the police, you know," I called out, making my way around behind him so he wouldn't see me. He spun round, trembling so hard that I was quite taken aback. When he realized it was me, he frowned.

"What the—? If it isn't Miss Furukura."

"Are you waiting in ambush? Causing a nuisance for customers is the taboo of all taboos for a store worker, you know."

"I'm not a store worker anymore."

"Well, I am, and I can't overlook this. The manager already warned you about it, didn't he? He's in the store now, so maybe I should go call him."

Shiraha straightened his back and stood up tall, looking down on me as if trying to intimidate me.

"What can a corporate slave loser like him do? I haven't done anything wrong. If I take a fancy to a certain woman, then I'll make her mine. Hasn't that always been the tradition between men and women, handed down since ancient times?"

"Shiraha, you said before that the *strongest* men get the women, didn't you? So you're contradicting yourself."

"True, I'm not working at the moment, but I've got a vision. Once I start my business, I'll have women flocking to me."

"Well then, wouldn't the proper way be for you to do that first? Then you'd be able to choose from all those women running after you?"

Shiraha looked down awkwardly. "Anyway, nothing's changed since the Stone Age. It's just that nobody realizes that. In the final analysis, we're all animals," he said, going off on a tangent. "If you ask me, this is a dysfunctional society. And since it's defective, I'm treated unfairly."

I thought he was probably right about that, and I couldn't even imagine what a perfectly functioning society would be like. I was beginning to lose track of what "society" actually was. I even had a feeling it was all an illusion.

Shiraha looked at me standing there in silence and suddenly pressed his hands to his face. I thought he was about to sneeze, but then I saw drops of water dripping through his fingers and realized he must be crying. It would be awful if we were spotted by any customers I thought. "Anyhow, let's go and sit down somewhere," I said, taking his arm and leading him to a nearby family restaurant.

* * *

"Our society doesn't allow any foreign objects. I've always suffered because of that," Shiraha said, drinking jasmine tea made with a teabag from the drink bar.

I was the one who had gotten the jasmine tea for him, since he didn't make any move to get anything for himself. He just sat in silence, and when I placed it in front of him, he started drinking it without even saying thank you.

"Everyone has to toe the line. Why am I still doing casual work even though I'm in my midthirties? Why haven't I ever had a girlfriend? The assholes don't even bat an eyelid when they ask whether I've ever had sex or not, and then they laugh and tell me not to include prostitutes in the count. I don't make trouble for anyone, but they all seem to think nothing of raping me just because I'm in the minority."

I considered him one step short of being a sex offender, but here he was casually likening his own suffering to sexual assault without sparing a thought for all the trouble he'd caused for women store workers and customers. He seemed to have this odd circuitry in his mind that allowed him to see himself only as the victim and never the perpetrator I thought as I watched him.

"Really?" I said, even wondering whether he made a habit of being self-pitying. "That must be hard."

I found society just as annoying as he did, but there wasn't anything about myself that I particularly wanted to defend, so I couldn't understand why Shiraha was taking it out on me like this. Well, I dare say life is tough for him, I thought, sipping at my warm water.

I hadn't added a teabag since I didn't really feel any need to drink flavored liquid.

"That's why I want to get married and be able to live without them bothering me all the time," Shiraha said. "I need someone with money. I have an idea for an online business. I don't want anyone copying my idea so I won't go into details, but ideally I want someone who can invest in it. My idea will definitely be a success, and when it is nobody will be able to moan at me anymore."

"So even though you hate people meddling in your life, you're deliberately choosing a lifestyle they won't be able to criticize?"

Surely that was tantamount to accepting society wholesale I thought, surprised.

"I'm tired," Shiraha said.

I nodded. "I suppose it is unreasonable to feel that way. If you can get them to stop complaining just by getting married, then that would be the simple and sensible thing to do, wouldn't it?"

"Don't make it sound so easy! We men have it much harder than women, you know. If you're not yet a fully fledged member of society, then it's get a job, and if you've got a job, it's earn more money, and if you earn more money, it's get married and have offspring. Society is continually judging us. Don't lump me together with women. You lot have a cushy time of it," he said sullenly.

"Well then, marriage won't solve anything then, will it? Isn't it pointless?" I said. But Shiraha didn't answer and carried on talking heatedly.

"I read history books trying to find out when society went so wrong. But however far back I went, a hundred years, two hundred years, a thousand years, it was always wrong. Even if you go back as far as the Stone Age!"

Shiraha banged his fist on the table, spilling jasmine tea from his cup.

"And so I realized. This society hasn't changed one bit. People who don't fit into the village are expelled: men who don't hunt, women who don't give birth to children. For all we talk about modern society and individualism, anyone who doesn't try to fit in can expect to be meddled with, coerced, and ultimately banished from the village."

"Shiraha, you do like talking about the Stone Age, don't you?"

"No, I don't like it. I hate it! But we live in a world that is basically the Stone Age with a veneer of contemporary society, you know. Strong men who bring home a good catch have women flocking around them, and they marry the prettiest girls in the village. Men who don't join in the hunt, or who are too weak to be of any use even if they try, are despised. The setup hasn't changed at all."

"Oh," I finally managed to say. But I couldn't say he was completely wrong. It was probably the same as the convenience store, where it was just us being continually replaced while the store remained the same unchanging scene.

This place really doesn't ever change, does it? The words of the old lady in the store echoed in my head.

"Furukura, how can you be so unfazed by it all? Aren't you ashamed of yourself?"

"What? Why?"

"You're still in a dead-end job at your age, and nobody's going to marry an old maid like you now.

You're like secondhand goods. Even if you are a virgin, you're grubby. You're like a Stone Age woman past childbearing age who can't get married and is left to just hang around the village, of no use to anyone, just a burden. I'm a man, so I can still make a comeback, but there's no hope for you, is there, Furukura?"

Up until now he'd been ranting about people meddling in his life, yet here he was attacking me with the same kinds of reproaches that were making him suffer. His argument was falling apart I thought. Maybe people who thought they were being violated felt a bit better when they attacked other people in the same way.

"And I wanted coffee!" he said petulantly, as if he'd only just noticed he was drinking jasmine tea. I stood up, went to the drink bar to pour some coffee, and placed it in front of him.

"Ugh. The coffee in places like this is awful."

"Shiraha, if all you want is a marriage of convenience, then how about getting together with me?" I broached as I put my second cup of warm water on the table and took a seat.

"What the—" he exploded.

"If you hate people interfering in your life so much and don't want to be kicked out of the village, then the sooner you get it over and done with the better, surely," I persisted. "I don't know about hunting—I mean, getting a job—but getting married will at least remove the risk of people sticking their noses into your love life and sexual history, won't it?"

"What the hell are you saying? That's ridiculous! I'm sorry, but there's no way I'll ever be able to get it up with you, Furukura."

"Get it up? Um, what has that got to do with marriage? Marriage is a matter of paperwork, an erection is a physiological phenomenon."

Shiraha kept quiet, so I explained further. "You're probably right about society being in the Stone Age. Anyone not needed in the village is persecuted and shunned. Ultimately, it's no different from a convenience store. Anyone the store doesn't need has their shifts reduced or is fired."

"What are you getting at?"

"To stay in a convenience store, you have to become a store worker. That's simple enough, you just wear a uniform and do as the manual says. And before you say anything, it was the same in Stone Age society, too. As long as you wear the skin of what's considered an ordinary person and follow the manual, you won't be driven out of the village or treated as a burden."

"I haven't a clue what you're blathering on about."

"In other words, you play the part of the fictitious creature called 'an ordinary person' that everyone has in them. Just like everyone in the convenience store is playing the part of the fictitious creature called 'a store worker.'"

"But that's painful. That's why I'm so bothered by it."

"Shiraha, until just a moment ago you were going along with it, weren't you? But when push comes to shove it's hard after all? Well, I guess anyone who devotes their life to fighting society in order to be free must be pretty sincere about suffering."

Shiraha glared at his coffee, apparently with nothing to say.

"But if it's that hard, there's really no need to go overboard. Unlike you, there are many things I don't really care about either way. It's just that since I don't have any particular purpose of my own, if the village wants things to be a certain way then I don't mind going along with that."

You eliminate the parts of your life that others find strange—maybe that's what everyone means when they say they want to "cure" me.

These past two weeks I'd been asked fourteen times why I wasn't married. And twelve times why I was still working part-time. So for now I'd decide what to eliminate from my life according to what I was asked about most often I thought.

Deep down I wanted some kind of change. Any change, whether good or bad, would be better than the state of impasse I was in now. Shiraha still didn't answer and just sat there staring solemnly at the coffee before him as if a hole had opened in its black surface.

*   *   *

Eventually I stood up and said, "I'll be off then." But then Shiraha started vaguely muttering things like: "You know, now that I think about it . . ." And more time went by as he droned on.

As his words haltingly came out, it became clear he was sharing an apartment but was in arrears with the rent and about to be kicked out. In the past, whenever he had to weather a situation he would go back to his parents' house in Hokkaido, but five years ago his younger brother had married and the house had been converted for the two families to live in together. Now that his brother's wife and their son were there, there was no place for him. Previously he'd always managed to wheedle money out of them, but his sister-in-law had apparently taken a dislike to him and he couldn't easily do that anymore.

"Since that bitch butted in, things have gotten weird. She's a fine one to talk, living off my brother like a parasite and lording it over everyone. She can fuck right off!"

He driveled on about himself, venting his pent-up resentment, and after a while I stopped listening and started looking at the clock.

It was already nearly eleven. I was working the next day, and I was running the risk of being short of sleep on the job. And as manager #2 had told me, my hourly pay covered the basic requirement to condition my body so it was fit to take to work.

"So, Shiraha, are you coming to my place? As long as you pay for food, you can stay there."

He didn't seem to have anywhere to go and would probably drag the conversation out until morning here by the restaurant's drinks bar if I let him. He started muttering "um . . ." and "well, but . . ." But I'd had enough and dragged him off back home with me.

Once we were in the confined space of my apartment, I realized that he stank, as though he'd been homeless for some time. I told him to have a bath and pushed him into the bathroom with a towel and shut the door. When I heard the sound of the shower, I breathed a sigh of relief.

He was in the bathroom for a long time, and I was falling asleep waiting for him when it suddenly occurred to me to call my sister.

"Hello?" came my sister's voice. It was barely this side of midnight, but she was apparently still up.

"Sorry to call so late. How's little Yutaro?"

"No problem. He's fast asleep, and I was just taking it easy. What's up?"

The vision of my nephew's face asleep there in my sister's house came to mind. My sister's life was progressing. At any rate, a living being that hadn't existed before was now there with her. Was she, like my mother, hoping for some change in my life? By way of an experiment, I decided to confess to her.

"It doesn't warrant calling you in the middle of the night, but . . . well, the truth is, there's a man in my home now."

"Eh!" Her voice sounded like it had come out the wrong way, more like a hiccup. I was about to ask if she was all right when she interrupted me, almost shouting in her confusion. "What, really? No kidding! Since when? What happened? What's he like?"

Overwhelmed by her onslaught, I answered, "Oh, not long. It's someone from work."

"Ah, I see. Congratulations!"

"Really?" I was a bit taken aback by her congratulating me without even asking for any more details.

"I don't know what he's like, but it's the first time you've ever said anything of the sort to me so, well . . . I'm so pleased for you! I'm behind you all the way."

"You are?"

"And the fact that you've reported it to me, does that by any chance mean you're already thinking about getting married? Oh, I'm sorry. Maybe I'm jumping the gun, here . . ."

She'd never been this chatty with me before. Seeing how excited she was, it occurred to me that it wasn't such a stretch to say that contemporary society was still stuck in the Stone Age after all. So the manual for life already existed. It was just that it was already ingrained in everyone's heads, and there wasn't any need to put it in writing. The specific form of what is considered an "ordinary person" had been there all along, unchanged since prehistoric times I finally realized.

"Keiko, I'm so happy for you. You've been struggling for so long, but at last you've found someone who understands . . ."

She was getting carried away with making up a story for herself. She might just as well have been saying I was "cured." If it had been that simple all along, I thought, I wish she'd given me clear instructions before, then I wouldn't have had to go to such lengths to find out how to be normal.

*   *   *

When I hung up, Shiraha was standing there looking lost.

"Oh, you don't have any change of clothes, do you? Use this. It's the uniform from when the store opened. I was given a new one when they changed the design. It's unisex, so it should fit okay."

Shiraha hesitated a moment, then he took the green top and put it on over his bare skin. His arms and legs were so long it looked a bit small on him, but at least he could close the zip. He only had a towel wound round his lower body, so I handed him some short pants I kept for wearing at home.

I didn't know how long it had been since Shiraha had last had a bath, but the underwear he'd just taken off stank to high heaven. For the time being I shoved them into the washing machine and told him to sit wherever he liked, so he warily sat down.

My apartment was the old-fashioned type consisting of one tatami room that opened onto a small kitchen, with separate bathroom and toilet. The fan didn't work very well, and after Shiraha came out of the bath, moisture and steam hung clammily in the room.

"It's a bit hot in here. Shall I open the window?"

"Um, well . . ."

Shiraha seemed restless and kept getting up and then sitting back down again.

"If you need the toilet, it's over there. It doesn't flush very well, so make sure you turn the lever all the way."

"Er, it's okay."

"So for the moment, you don't have anywhere to go, do you? You've pretty much been kicked out of your shared apartment."

"Ah."

"I've been thinking. You know, it might actually be convenient for me to have you here. I called my sister just now to see what her reaction would be, and she immediately jumped to her own conclusion and was really happy for me. It appears that if a man and a woman are alone in an apartment together, people's imaginations run wild and they're satisfied regardless of the reality."

"You called your sister?" Shiraha looked perplexed.

"Do you want a can of coffee? There's also lemonade. I only bought dented cans, though, and they're not cold."

"Dented cans?"

"Oh, hasn't anybody explained that to you before? When cans have a dent in them they're damaged goods and can't be sold to the public. Other than that, there's only milk or hot water."

"Oh. I'll have a can of coffee."

The only furniture in my room is a small folding table. I hadn't put my futon away, so I rolled it up and pushed it up against the refrigerator to make more space. I have another set of bedding in the closet for when my mother or sister comes to stay.

"I've got another futon, so you can stay here for the time being if you don't have anywhere to go. It's a bit cramped, though."

"Stay?" He fidgeted nervously. "Er, well, but . . . I'm a stickler for cleanliness, so . . . unless I'm properly prepared, um . . ." he said in a small voice.

"If cleanliness is a problem, then you're probably not going to like the futon. It hasn't been used for a while and hasn't been hung out to air. And this is an old apartment, so there are loads of cockroaches."

"Oh well that's not . . . I mean the apartment I was sharing wasn't particularly clean and that doesn't bother me, but still . . . I mean, I feel a bit like I'm being presented with a fait accompli or something . . . Look, as a man I have to be on my guard. Phoning your sister out of the blue like that, it's a bit pushy isn't it?"

"Did I do something wrong? I only wanted to see her reaction."

"Uh, I mean, that in itself is a bit scary. I've read about this sort of thing online, but I never really thought it happened in real life. Being coerced into staying like that kind of turns me off . . ."

"What? I just thought you didn't have anywhere else to go! If I'm causing trouble for you, then it's fine for you to leave. I haven't turned the washing machine on yet, so I can give you your clothes back."

"Oh, but," he mumbled. "If you insist . . ."

I couldn't make head or tail of what he was saying, and the conversation obviously wasn't going anywhere.

"Um, I'm sorry but it's getting late," I said. "Do you mind if I go to sleep? If you want to leave then go ahead, or if you want to stay then get the futon and lay it out yourself. Do as you please. I have an early start at the convenience store tomorrow morning. Sixteen years ago I learned from manager #2 that my pay covers the basic requirement to manage my life so that

I'm fit for work. I must get enough sleep before going to work."

"Ah, the convenience store . . ." Shiraha said inanely.

If I paid him any more attention it would end up being morning, so I went ahead and laid out my own futon.

"I'm tired," I told him. "I'll get up early and take a bath in the morning. I'll probably make a bit of noise, but don't mind me."

I brushed my teeth and set my alarm clock, then got in my futon and closed my eyes. Now and then I heard a rustling sound coming from Shiraha, but gradually the sound of the convenience store grew louder in my head and before I knew it I was being drawn into sleep.

* * *

The next morning when I woke up, Shiraha was fast asleep with his lower body stuck in the closet. He didn't stir even when I went into the bathroom.

I left home in time to reach the store by 8:00 a.m. as usual, leaving him a note: *If you go out, please leave the key in the mailbox.*

He'd sounded like he was only reluctantly staying in my apartment, so I wasn't really expecting him to be there when I got home, but he was.

He wasn't doing anything, simply sitting with his elbows on the folding table, drinking a dented can of white grape soda.

"So you're still here."

He jumped at the sound of my voice. "Uh . . ."

"My sister has been e-mailing me all day. It's the first time I've ever seen her get so excited about something to do with me."

"It's hardly surprising. Even your sister would think it more respectable for a virgin left on the shelf to be living with a man rather than still working in a convenience store at a ripe old age."

He was back to his usual self, with no trace of the discomfort he'd shown last night.

"Oh . . . so you don't think I'm respectable either?"

"Look, anyone who doesn't fit in with the village loses any right to privacy. They'll trample all over you as they please. You either get married and have kids or go hunting and earn money, and anyone who doesn't contribute to the village in one of these forms is a heretic.

And the villagers will come poking their noses into your life as much as they want."

"Ah."

"You need to wake up, Furukura. To put it bluntly, you're the lowest of the low. Your womb is probably too old to be of any use, and you don't even have the looks to serve as a means to satisfy carnal desire. But then neither are you earning money like a man. Far from it, you're only working part-time without even a proper job. Frankly speaking, you're just a burden on the village, the dregs of society."

"I see. But I'm not capable of working anywhere else except the convenience store. I did give it a go, but it turns out the convenience store worker mask is the only one I'm fit to wear. So if people don't accept that, I have no idea what I can do about it."

"That's why contemporary society is dysfunctional. They might mumble nice things about diversity of lifestyles and whatnot, but in the end nothing has changed since prehistoric times. With the birthrate in decline, society is regressing rapidly to the Stone Age, and it's going beyond life just being uncomfortable. Society has reached the stage in which not being of any use to the village means being condemned just for existing."

Shiraha wasn't just picking on me; he was openly expressing his fury against society. I wasn't sure which of us he was angrier with. He seemed to be just throwing out words randomly at whatever happened to be in his sights.

"Furukura, I thought your proposal was crazy, but actually it's not a bad idea. I may be able to help you out. If I'm in your apartment, everyone will probably look down on you for living with a pauper, but they'll at least be content, whereas they can't get their heads around you the way you are now. Without a career or a husband, you're of no value to society, and people like you get expurgated from the village."

"Uh-huh."

"Back at the store, I was angling for marriage, sure, but you're far from being my ideal marriage partner, Furukura. You don't earn much working in a convenience store, which means I won't be able to start my own business, and I won't even be able to satisfy my sexual needs with someone like you."

Shiraha downed the last of the dented can of soda as if he were knocking back a shot.

"But having said that, our interests do coincide, so I don't mind staying here."

"Ah."

I took a can of chocolate-melon soda from a paper bag full of dented cans and handed it to him.

"Um, so what's in it for you, Shiraha?"

He was quiet for a few moments, then said in a small voice: "I want you to hide me."

"What?"

"I want you to keep me hidden from society. I don't mind you using my existence here for your own ends, and you can talk about me all you want. I myself want to spend all my time hiding here. I've had enough of complete strangers poking their noses into my business."

Shiraha sipped on his chocolate-melon soda without looking up.

"If I go out, my life will be violated again. When you're a man, it's all 'go to work' and 'get married.' And once you're married, then it's 'earn more' and 'have children'! You're a slave to the village. Society orders you to work your whole life. Even my testicles are the property of the village! Just by having no sexual experience they treat you as though you're wasting your semen."

"I can see how stressful that would be."

"Your uterus belongs to the village too, you know. The only reason the villagers aren't paying it any attention is because it's useless. I want to spend my whole life doing nothing. For my whole life, until I die, I want to just breathe without anyone interfering in my life. That's all I wish for," he finished, holding his palms together as if in supplication.

I was considering whether there was any benefit to me in having him here. My mother and sister, and even I myself, were beginning to tire of me never being cured. I was beginning to feel that any change, good or bad, would be better than my situation now.

"It probably isn't as tough for me as it is for you, Shiraha. But one thing's for sure: I won't be able to carry on working in the convenience store like this forever. Every time a new manager comes along, they ask me why I've only ever done the same part-time job. They're always suspicious until I give them some kind of excuse. And I was just looking for a good excuse to be able to give them. I don't know if you're it, though."

"As long as I'm here, society will be satisfied. For you it's a good deal all around."

He seemed very confident about it. His insistence made me dubious, even though I'd been the one to propose it. Then again, when I recalled my sister's reaction and the expression on the faces of Miho and the others when I told them I'd never been in love, I thought maybe it really wouldn't hurt to give it a go.

"I said 'a deal,' but remuneration won't be necessary. It'll be enough if you just keep me here and provide me with meals."

"Ah. Well, I suppose there's not much point in me demanding payment from you if you're not earning anything. I'm poor too, so I can't give you any money. But if you're not fussy I can provide your feed for you."

"What?"

"Oh, sorry. It's the first time I've kept an animal at home, so it feels like having a pet, you see."

Shiraha looked annoyed at my turn of phrase but said smugly, "Well, that should do." Then he added, "Talking of food, I haven't eaten anything since morning."

"Oh, right, there's some leftovers in the refrigerator, so please help yourself."

I took out some plates and laid the table, placing some cooked rice and boiled vegetables seasoned with soy sauce in the middle.

Shiraha frowned. "What's this?"

"Daikon radish, bean sprouts, potatoes, and rice."

"Do you always eat this sort of thing?"

"This sort of thing?"

"Cooking isn't exactly your strong point, is it?"

"I just heat-treat the food before eating it. I don't particularly need to taste it, but if I need to up my salt intake I add soy sauce."

I explained it clearly for him, but he didn't seem to understand. Reluctantly taking a forkful to his mouth, he snapped, "It *is* like dog food!"

Of course it is, I thought. That's why I said that. I stuck my fork into a piece of daikon and put it in my mouth.

*   *   *

I'd kind of sensed that I was taking in a fraud when I let Shiraha come to live with me, but his predictions turned out to be surprisingly accurate. It *was* convenient to have him around. It didn't take long for me to be convinced.

After my sister, the next time I mentioned him to anyone was at a gathering at Miho's place. We were all sitting around eating cake when I casually let it drop that he was living with me.

They were all so ecstatic about it that I even had to wonder whether they'd lost their minds.

"Wait, what? Since when?"

"What's he like?"

"Wow, that's amazing! I was so worried about what would become of you, Keiko. I'm really so pleased for you!"

"Thank you," I said simply, feeling a bit weirded out by how jubilant they all were.

"Come on, tell us about him. What's his job? What does he do?"

"He doesn't do anything. He did say he had a dream to set up his own business, but it seems to have been all talk. He just loafs about at home."

They all leaned forward, suddenly serious.

"Yes! Some men are like that . . . but they tend to be kinder and more sincere, and charming, right? My friend fell in love with a guy like that, although I can't say what's so good about him myself."

"A friend of mine on the rebound from an affair got involved with a guy who used to live off her. If he'd done some housework you could at least have said he was like a housewife, but he never even lifted a finger. But his attitude completely changed when she got pregnant, and now they look really happy."

"Yes, absolutely! Getting pregnant is the best thing to do with that kind of man."

Everyone seemed happier than when I'd told them I'd never been in love, and they were carrying on as if they knew everything about my situation. The previous me—who'd never fallen in love or had sex, who'd never had a proper job—had sometimes been hard to read. But everything about the new me—the one who had Shiraha living with her—was clear, even my future.

Listening to my friends go on about me and Shiraha was like hearing them talk about a couple of total strangers. They seemed to have the story wrapped up between them. It was about characters who had the same names as we did, but who had absolutely nothing to do with me or Shiraha.

When I tried to interrupt them I was told: "Look, just take our advice!" "Yes, that's right. After all, you're a novice at falling in love, Keiko. We've heard so much about this type of guy that we're sick to death of 'em!" "You went out with someone like that when you were young too, didn't you Miho?" They were all enjoying themselves so much I decided not to volunteer any more information than I was specifically asked for.

It was as though everyone was saying that for the first time I was part of their circle. I had the feeling they were all welcoming me on board.

Painfully aware that until now they'd evidently thought of me as an outsider, I listened to them carry on excitedly, merely nodding brightly and occasionally muttering "I see" in the same tone Sugawara always used.

*   *   *

After I adopted Shiraha, things went even more smoothly for me at the convenience store. But feeding him did cost me more money. Fridays and Sundays had always been my days off, but the thought of asking to work these shifts too actually added more spring to my step.

I finished tidying up the trash bins outside and went into the back room. The manager had just come off the night shift and was making up the work roster, so I nonchalantly broached the matter with him.

"Um, have you already filled the shifts for Friday and Sunday? I'm trying to save up, so I'd be happy to work more shifts."

"Attagirl, Miss Furukura! Always so full of enthusiasm. But I'd be breaking the law to have you work the whole week without a day off, you know. How about getting another job on the side? All the stores are shorthanded, so I'm sure they'll be delighted."

"Thanks, it'd be a great help."

"Take care not to make yourself sick, eh? Oh, here, your pay slip for the month," he said, passing me my salary statement.

I was just putting it in my bag when I heard him sigh and mutter, "Ah, I have to get Shiraha's to him too. He hasn't picked up his belongings yet either, and I can't get hold of him."

"What, can't you get through to his phone?"

"It rings, but he doesn't answer. He really is hopeless. I told him not to bring his personal effects into work, but he did and now there's a lot still left in the locker."

"Shall I take them to him?"

A new guy was due to start on the night shift. I thought it would be a problem if the locker was still full, and it just slipped out.

"What? You mean take it to Shiraha?" he asked in surprise. "What's this all about, Miss Furukura? Are you in touch with him?"

Oops, I thought and nodded.

I don't mind you talking about me to people who don't know me, but I don't want you to let anyone at the convenience store know I'm here. That's what Shiraha had said.

I want you to hide me from everyone who knows me. I haven't caused any trouble for anyone, but they all think nothing of poking their noses into my life. I just want to exist, quietly breathing.

I was just recalling him muttering this under his breath when the automatic door chime sounded through the security monitor. I looked at the screen to see a group of male customers coming in. All at once the store was busy. Tuan, the new guy who'd started only last week, was alone on the cash register, so I thought I'd better get out there right away to help.

"Hey, hey, not so fast. You can't get away that easily!" the store manager yelled, amused.

I pointed at the screen. "He needs help on the till," I told him, and I rushed out into the shop.

There were three customers waiting by the time I got there, and Tuan was looking flustered as he operated the till.

"Um, what do I do with this?"

Apparently he wasn't sure how to process a voucher. I dealt with it quickly and told him: "This is a money-back voucher. Give them their change, okay?" Then I rushed to the other till.

"Sorry to keep you waiting! Next customer over here, please."

A man who was looking a bit disgruntled at having been kept waiting came over and said irritably, "Is that guy new? I'm in a hurry."

"I'm so sorry!" I said and bowed my head.

Tuan wasn't used to working the tills yet, and Mrs. Izumi should have been keeping an eye on him. I looked around and saw she was busy putting in an order for carton drinks, apparently unaware there were so many customers waiting to pay.

When things finally calmed down on the cash register, I noticed that the deep-fried chicken skewers for today's promotion hadn't been made yet so I hastily ran to get some from the back room freezer.

The manager and Mrs. Izumi were in the back room talking about something, looking amused.

"We were aiming for a hundred chicken skewers today, weren't we? But there aren't any ready for the lunchtime rush yet, and the POP ad hasn't been put out either!" I told them.

I'd expected them both to respond, "Oh no, that's terrible!" But Mrs. Izumi just leaned over to me and said, "Hey, Miss Furukura, what's all this I hear about you and Shiraha? Is it true?"

"What? But Mrs. Izumi, the skewers—"

"Just a moment, how long has this been going on? You're a good match though! Come on, tell us. Which one of you made the first move? Was it Shiraha?"

"Oh, she's too embarrassed to let anything on . . . We'll have to take her out drinking sometime. Make sure you bring Shiraha too, Furukura!"

"But, the skewers!"

"Stop avoiding the subject! Come on, tell us!"

Irritated, I yelled at them: "Look, it isn't that there's anything between us! He's just staying at my place now, that's all. What's important is that we haven't even started preparing the chicken skewers yet!"

"What?" Mrs. Izumi screeched. "You mean you're *living* together?"

"Seriously?" put in the manager.

They sounded so excited I decided it was useless saying anything more and rushed over to the freezer, took out the boxes of chicken skewers, and ran with my arms full back to the cash register.

I was shocked by their reaction. As a convenience store worker, I couldn't believe they were putting gossip about store workers before a promotion in which chicken skewers that usually sold at 130 yen were to be put on sale at the special price of 110 yen. What on earth had happened to the pair of them?

Tuan must have noticed how rattled I looked as I rushed in with the boxes, because he came over to help me with them.

"Wow, a lot! You make all?" he asked in his broken Japanese.

"That's right. They're on promotion. We're aiming to sell a hundred today. Last time we managed ninety-one, so we can reach the goal! Sawaguchi from the evening shift made us a big POP ad to use today. If all the staff rally around, we can sell them. That's what's most important for this store right now," I said, getting all choked up for some reason.

"Rally?" he queried, his head on one side, unable to follow my rapid-fire Japanese.

"Look, we have to work together to pull it off! Tuan, please, get all of these ready now!"

"All? Oh wow!" he said, nodding, and clumsily started to prepare them.

I ran over to the fast-food display case and began setting up the three-dimensional POP ad Sawaguchi had spent at least two hours of overtime on. It was made from cardboard and colored drawing paper and read: TODAY'S TOP PICK! JUICY FRIED-CHICKEN SKEWERS FOR 110 YEN! TODAY ONLY!

I got on the stepladder and hung the POP ad from the ceiling, where it looked spectacular. Sawaguchi had said as she was making it that with this to help us, we'd definitely manage to sell a hundred skewers.

All of us store workers were pitching in to achieve our common goal, so what on earth did the manager and Mrs. Izumi think they were doing?

"Irasshaimasé! Good morning!" I called out as a customer came into the store. "Deep-fried chicken skewers are on offer today for just a hundred and ten yen! How about it?"

Tuan was just arranging the skewers that were done, and he raised his voice alongside mine. "Fried-chicken skewers! How about it?"

The manager and Mrs. Izumi still hadn't come out of the back room. I thought I could hear the faint sound of Mrs. Izumi's laugh.

"They're cheap! Fried-chicken skewers! Try one!"

Tuan might not yet be used to the work, but he alone was a valued colleague as he joined me in trying to entice the customers to buy today's special.

*   *   *

On the way home I stopped off at the local supermarket to buy some bean sprouts, chicken, and cabbage, but when I got home Shiraha was nowhere to be seen.

I started preparing to boil the food, thinking that maybe he'd left, when I heard a noise coming from the bathroom.

"Oh, is that you, Shiraha?"

I opened the bathroom door to find him sitting fully dressed in the dry bathtub watching movies on his tablet.

"Why are you in here?"

"I tried the closet first, but there are bugs in there, you know. There aren't any bugs in here, so I can relax," he answered. "Is it boiled vegetables again today?"

"Yes, that's right. Today I'm heat-treating bean sprouts, chicken, and cabbage."

"Oh, okay," he said, without looking up. "You're home late today, aren't you? I'm hungry."

"I was about to leave when the manager and Mrs. Izumi started talking to me and wouldn't let me go. The manager was at the store all day even though it was his day off. He was going on and on at me to bring you out drinking one evening."

"What? You told them about me?"

"I'm sorry. It just slipped out. Oh, here. I brought you your belongings and your latest pay slip."

"Oh." Shiraha clutched his tablet without saying anything for a while. Then: "You told them . . . even though I told you not to."

"I'm sorry. I didn't mean any harm."

"You've gone and done it now, Furukura."

"What?" I looked at him, puzzled.

"The bastards are going to do their best to drag me out so they can lecture me. But I'm not going. No way. I'm going to stay hidden here. Which means you're next on the list for the lecture, Furukura."

"I am?"

"Why are you letting an unemployed man live in your apartment? It's okay for both husband and wife to work, but not in a casual job! Aren't you going to get married? What about children? Get a proper job! Fulfill your role as an adult! They're all going to be on your back now, you know."

"Nobody in the store has ever talked to me like that before."

"That's because you're just too far out there. A thirty-six-year-old, single convenience store worker, probably a virgin at that, zealously working every day, shouting at the top of her lungs, full of energy. Yet showing no signs of looking for a proper job. You're a foreign object. It's just nobody bothered to tell you because they find you too freaky. They've been saying it behind your back, though. And now they'll start saying it to your face too."

"What?"

"People who are considered normal enjoy putting those who aren't on trial, you know. But if you kick me out now, they'll judge you even more harshly, so you have no choice but to keep me around." Shiraha gave a thin laugh. "I always did want revenge, on women who are allowed to become parasites just because they're women. I always thought to myself that I'd be a parasite one day. That'd show them. And I'm going to be a parasite on you, Furukura, whatever it takes."

I didn't have a clue what he was going on about.

"Well anyway, what about your feed? I put it on to boil, and it should be done now."

"I'll eat it here. Bring it to me, please."

I did as he said and put the boiled vegetables and white rice on a plate and took it into the bathroom.

"Close the door behind you, will you?"

I did as he said and closed the bathroom door. I sat down alone at the table for the first time in a while and started to eat.

The sound of my chewing was extraordinarily loud. It was probably because I'd been surrounded by the sounds of the convenience store until shortly before.

When I closed my eyes and pictured the store, in my mind its sounds came back to life.

That sound flowed through me like music. Swaying to the sounds etched deep within me of the store performing, of the store operating, I stuffed the food before me into my body so that I would be fit to work again tomorrow.

*   *   *

The news about Shiraha spread through the store like wildfire. Every time I saw the manager he started pestering me with: "How's Shiraha? When are you going to bring him out drinking with us?"

I'd always had a lot of respect for manager #8. He was a hard worker and I'd thought of him as the perfect colleague, but now I was sick to death of him only ever talking about Shiraha whenever we met.

Until now, we'd always had meaningful worker-manager discussions: "It's been hot lately, so the sales of chocolate desserts are down," or "There's a new block of flats down the road, so we've been getting more customers in the evening," or "They're really pushing the ad campaign for that new product coming out the week after next, so we should do well with it." Now, however, it felt like he'd downgraded me from store worker to female of the human species.

"Miss Furukura, if there's anything you're worried about, I don't mind lending an ear!" he would say. "And of course, you must come out for a drink with us next time, even if you do come alone. Although it'd be better if Shiraha came too. I'd soon talk some sense into him!"

Even Sugawara, who'd always hated Shiraha, chimed in with: "I want to see him too! Do bring him along!"

I'd never known before now, but apparently they all went out socializing together now and then. Even Mrs. Izumi sometimes joined them when her husband could look after the children.

"You know, I always did want to go out with you too sometime, Miss Furukura!"

So they were all scheming how to drag Shiraha out with them one night, to give him a good talking-to. I was beginning to understand why he wanted to hide himself away, if this was what he had to put up with when he went out.

The manager even brought out Shiraha's CV, which should have been disposed of when he left, and together with Mrs. Izumi started picking it apart.

"Look here. He dropped out of university and went to technical school, and then he dropped out of that too!"

"So his only qualification to speak of is the English Proficiency Test? And he doesn't even have a driver's license!"

They were all having fun putting him down. They evidently thought he was more important than the current promotion with all rice balls on sale at a hundred yen, and the cheese frankfurters that had just arrived in the store, and the discount vouchers on all precooked dishes that we now had for handing out to customers.

It was like there was noise interference mixed in with the sound of the store. It was a hideous cacophony—as though everyone had been playing the same score, but had suddenly pulled out random instruments and begun playing them instead.

The scariest thing of all, though, was the newest employee, Tuan. He was rapidly absorbing the store and beginning to resemble all the other workers. That wouldn't have mattered in the previous version of the store, but with everyone in their current weird state, it was as though he were transforming into a creature that was nothing like a store worker.

He'd been such a hard worker, but now he stopped cooking the frankfurters and asked, "Your husband work here before, Miss Furukura?" He was now speaking with a hint of Mrs. Izumi's drawl.

"He's not my husband," I answered quickly. "And more to the point, it's hot today, so we'll be selling lots of cold drinks. Please be sure to restock the bottles of mineral water from the cardboard box in the walk-in refrigerator. Cartons of cold green tea will sell well too, so do keep an eye on those shelves, okay?"

"You going to have a baby, Miss Furukura? My sister is married with three kids. They're still small and so cute."

Tuan was rapidly ceasing to be a store worker. It was the same with all of them. Even though they still wore the same uniform and did the same work, I had the feeling they were less like store workers than they had been before.

Only the customers remained unchanged and continued to need me to be a perfect store worker for them.

I'd thought the rest of the staff was made up of the same cells as me, but in the current strange atmosphere a village mentality was taking over and they were fast reverting to ordinary males and females. Now only the customers still allowed me to be just a convenience store worker.

*　*　*

One Sunday, a month after I'd called her, my sister turned up to lecture Shiraha.

She is generally a sweet, gentle person, but she was extremely tense as she demanded to come in. "I have to say something. It's for your own good, Keiko," she said.

I told Shiraha he could wait outside, but he merely said, "It's okay. I don't mind," apparently resolved to stay in the apartment. This was surprising, given how much he hated being raked over the coals.

"My husband is looking after Yutaro. As well he should, from time to time," she said as she came in the door.

"I see. It's a bit cramped in here, but make yourself at home."

It was the first time in ages I'd seen her without her son, and she looked as though she'd somehow mislaid something.

"You didn't have to come all the way over here. If you'd called me, I'd have gone to your apartment as usual."

"It's okay. Today I wanted to take my time talking to you. I'm not disturbing you, am I?" She glanced around the room. "Oh, but what about the guy living with you? Is he out today? I hope I didn't scare him off."

"What? No, he's here."

"Oh! But where is he? I must say hello!" she said, jumping up.

"Don't worry about it. There's really no need. Oh, but it's about feeding time anyway." I took some boiled potatoes and cabbage from the cooking pan and put them along with some rice into a washbasin I kept in the kitchen and took it to the bathroom.

Shiraha was sitting on cushions he'd stuffed into the bathtub and fiddling with his smartphone. I held his feed out for him, and he took it.

"The bathroom? Is he in the bath?"

"Yes, it's really cramped when we're together in the room, so I'm keeping him in there." My sister looked incredulous, so I explained further. "I mean, this apartment is really old, isn't it? Shiraha says that taking a coin-pay shower is better than getting into such an old bath. He gives me small change to cover the cost of my shower and his feed. It's a bit of a hassle, but it's convenient having him here. Everyone's really happy for me. They're all congratulating me. They've all convinced themselves my new situation is great, and they've stopped poking their nose into my business. So he's useful."

She looked down. Maybe this time she finally got it, now that I'd explained it carefully to her.

"Oh, by the way, I bought some custard puddings that were past their sell date. Do you want one?"

"I never imagined it was anything like this," she said, her voice trembling.

Surprised, I looked at her and saw she appeared to be crying.

"What's wrong? Oh, I'll go get some tissues!" I said immediately, using Sugawara's speech style. Then I stood up.

"Will you *ever* be cured, Keiko . . . ?" She looked down, not even bothering to remonstrate with me. "I simply can't take it anymore. How can we make you normal? How much longer must I put up with this?"

"What? You've been putting up with me? If that's the case, you needn't have gone to all the trouble of coming to see me, surely?" I told her honestly.

She stood up, tears pouring down her face. "Keiko, won't you come to see a counselor with me? Please? Let's get you help. It's the only way."

"I went to see one when I was little, but it didn't do any good, did it? And I don't even know what it is I need to be cured of."

"Ever since you started working at the convenience store, you've gotten weirder and weirder. The way you talk, the way you yell out at home as if you were still in the store, and even your facial expressions are weird. I'm begging you. Please try to be normal!" She began crying even harder.

"So, will I be cured if I leave the convenience store? Or am I better staying working there? And should I kick Shiraha out? Or am I better with him here? Look, I'll do whatever you say. I don't mind either way, so please just instruct me in specific terms."

"I don't know anymore . . ."

She kept crying uncontrollably without responding to my request. Lost for something to do I took a custard pudding out of the refrigerator and ate it as I watched her sitting there sobbing.

Just then there was the sound of the bathroom door opening. I turned in surprise and saw Shiraha standing there.

"I'm so sorry. To tell you the truth, your sister and I just had a fight. I made a real embarrassing spectacle of myself, didn't I? You must be really shocked."

I stared openmouthed at him. It wasn't at all like him to be such a smooth talker.

"The fact is that I'd connected with my ex-girlfriend on Facebook and we went out drinking together. Keiko was furious when she found out. She refused to let me sleep with her and shut me in the bathroom."

My sister stared at him for a while as if mulling over the meaning of what he was saying. Then she clutched hold of him and stood up, her face the picture of a believer who had just come across the priest in church.

"So *that's* what happened . . . I see, so that's it!"

"And when I heard you were on your way up to the apartment, I thought I'd better keep out of the way. I didn't want to be lectured to."

"Yes . . . absolutely! When I heard from my sister that you're just loafing around without a job, I was worried that she was being duped by some weirdo . . . but now I hear you're unfaithful too! That's really inexcusable!"

She looked as happy as happy can be as she started laying into him.

So that was it: now that she thinks he's "one of us" she can lecture him. She's far happier thinking her sister is normal, even if she has a lot of problems, than she is having an abnormal sister for whom everything is fine. For her, normality—however messy—is far more comprehensible.

"As Keiko's sister, I have to tell you that I really am furious with you, Shiraha!"

I noticed that her way of speaking had shifted slightly. What kind of people was she surrounding herself with these days? I was willing to bet that the way she was speaking now resembled their speech patterns.

"I know. I am looking for work, although it's going slowly, and of course we're thinking in terms of getting married soon."

"As things stand now, it goes without saying that I can't possibly inform our parents of the relationship!"

It appeared I'd reached my limit. Nobody wanted me to continue being a store worker.

My sister had been delighted when I started the job, but now she was saying that leaving it was the normal thing to do. She had dried her tears, but her nose was running and her upper lip was wet. Yet she was so carried away lambasting Shiraha that she didn't even wipe it. I stared at the two of them, half-eaten pudding in my hand, unable even to wipe my sister's nose for her.

*   *   *

The next day I came home from work to see some red shoes in the entrance hall.

I went inside wondering whether my sister had come back or even whether Shiraha had maybe brought a girlfriend home with him, but he was kneeling formally with his back straight as he faced a brown-haired woman who was glaring at him across the table.

"Um . . . may I ask who you are?"

The woman abruptly looked up at the sound of my voice. She was still young, her makeup on the heavy side.

"Are you the one who's living with him now?"

"Er, yes, that's right."

"I'm his younger brother's wife. We got a call from his roommate after he ran away without paying his rent and refused to answer any calls. He ignores any calls from us too. I just happened to be coming to Tokyo for an alumni reunion, so I paid the outstanding rent on behalf of my mother-in-law and apologized for all the trouble he has caused. I always knew it would come to this, you know. He's always been greedy and careless with money. And he has absolutely no intention of working for a living. But I swear I'll make him pay it all back to me."

On the table between them was a piece of paper marked IOU.

"Get a job and pay it all back! I really don't see why I should have to go to so much effort for my brother-in-law."

"Um . . . how did you know I was here?" Shiraha asked in a small voice.

One of the reasons Shiraha had asked me to hide him was because he'd run away without paying the rent I realized.

She snorted with laughter at his question. "You've been late with rent and come home to borrow money before, haven't you? I realized then that it was only a matter of time before something like this happened, and so I got my husband to install a tracking app on your cell phone. That's how I knew where to find you. All I had to do was lay in wait until you popped out to do some shopping."

It struck me that she really didn't trust him one bit.

"I'll pay you back . . . Really, I will," he said, hanging his head.

"You're telling me you will. And what is your relationship with this woman?" she asked, turning to look at me. "How come you're living together if you haven't even got a job? If you've got time for that, then you've got time to work. So go out and get a real job. You're an adult, after all."

"We're in a relationship and plan to get married. We've decided that she works, while I look after the home. Once her place of employment is decided, I'll repay the money from her salary."

Oh, so he has a girlfriend I thought, but then remembered the exchange between him and my sister yesterday and realized he was referring to me.

"Is that so? What job are you doing now?" she asked, giving me a skeptical look.

"Oh, um, I'm working in a convenience store," I answered.

She gaped at me, her eyes, nostrils, and mouth all forming O's. I was just recalling having seen a face just like that before when she virtually screamed at me: "What! And you two are living together? When this man doesn't even have a job?"

"Um . . . yes."

"It's not as if you can carry on like this, though, is it? You'll wear yourself out! I mean, look, I'm sorry if I'm being rude, but you're not exactly a spring chicken, are you? How come you haven't got a proper job?"

"Well . . . I did attend a few interviews, but the convenience store was the only place I was able to work in."

She stared at me aghast. "In a way you kind of suit each other, but . . . Look, I know it's none of my business, but you should really either get a job or get married, one or the other. I mean, seriously. Or better still, you should do both. Otherwise you're going to end up starving to death sometime, you know. You're really living on the edge."

"I see."

"For the life of me I don't know what you see in this guy, but if you really are in love with him that's even more reason for you to get a proper job. No way can two social dropouts survive on just one store worker's wage. I'm serious!"

"Okay."

"Hasn't anyone else told you this before? And what about health insurance? Are you even registered? I'm only bringing this up for your own sake, you know! We've only just met, so maybe it isn't my place to be saying all this, but for your own good you really should get your life in order."

Seeing her leaning in close and taking the trouble to speak to me like this, I felt she was much nicer than Shiraha had made out.

"We've discussed all this. Until we have children, I will take care of the home and concentrate on setting up an online business. Once we have a child, I'll go out to work and be the breadwinner of the family."

"Stop babbling nonsense and just get a real job, will you? Well, it's up to the two of you and I suppose I shouldn't be poking my nose into your business, but—"

"I've told her to leave the convenience store right away and focus on looking for a proper job. We already made that decision ourselves."

Eh? I thought with a start.

"I suppose just the fact you have a partner is something of an improvement," she said rather reluctantly. "Anyway, I don't want to overstay my welcome, so I'll be going now." She stood up. "I'll tell your mother about today's events, including how much money we've lent you, so don't think you're going to get away with it, all right?"

And with that, she left.

Shiraha listened intently to the sound of the door closing and the departing footsteps of his sister-in-law. Once he was certain she had gone, he gave a whoop of delight. "I did it! I got away! Everything's okay for the time being. There's no way you'll be getting pregnant, no chance of me ever penetrating a woman like you, after all."

He grabbed me by my shoulders in his excitement. "Furukura, you're lucky, you know. Thanks to me, you can go from being triply handicapped as a single, virgin convenience store worker to being a married member of society. Everyone will assume you're a sexually active, respectable human being. That's the image of you that pleases them most. Isn't it wonderful?"

Having been caught up in Shiraha's family matters the moment I got back from work, I was dead tired and not in the mood to listen to him blather on.

"Um, can I use my shower for once today?"

He took the futon out of the bathtub, and for the first time in weeks I showered at home instead of having to go out to the coin-operated shower. Meanwhile he stood outside the bathroom door talking nonstop. "You're so lucky you met me, Furukura. If you'd gone on like before you'd have ended up dying alone and destitute. Far better you keep on hiding me forever!"

His voice receded and all I could hear was the water as it slowly drowned out any last traces of the convenience store sounds left in my ears.

As I finished rinsing the soap from my body and turned the faucet tightly shut, my ears heard silence for the first time in a long time.

Until now, the convenience store had always been ringing in my ears. But now those sounds were gone.

The long-forgotten silence sounded like music I'd never heard before. As I stood stock-still listening to this, it was split by the sound of the floor creaking under Shiraha's weight.

*   *   *

All too quickly, as if the eighteen years of my employment had been just an illusion, my last day at the convenience store arrived.

I went to the store at 6:00 a.m. and spent the time watching the security camera monitor.

Tuan was now accustomed to the cash register and quickly scanned cans of coffee and sandwiches with a practiced air, smoothly providing a receipt whenever requested.

We were supposed to give a month's notice of quitting, but given the circumstances they were letting me go after only two weeks.

I recalled the manager's reaction two weeks earlier when I told him I wanted to leave.

"Really? At last! So Shiraha's acting like a man after all, is he?"

He had always been put out by people leaving since it left him shorthanded, and he always demanded they help find a replacement. This time, however, he seemed over the moon. Maybe no genuine store managers existed anywhere anymore. Before me now was a human male, mindlessly hoping that one of the same species was going to breed.

Mrs. Izumi, who had always commented indignantly on the lack of professionalism shown by people leaving suddenly, also congratulated me. "I heard all about it! I'm so happy for you!"

I took off my uniform and removed my name badge, and I handed them to the manager.

"Well then, thank you for everything."

"We're going to miss you, Miss Furukura! Thanks for all your hard work."

I'd worked there for eighteen years, and then it was over just like that. In my place, the new girl from Myanmar who'd started last week was already on the cash register scanning bar codes. I looked at the security camera monitor out of the corner of my eye and thought to myself that I would never be shown on it again.

"Miss Furukura, really, thank you so much for working here!"

Mrs. Izumi and Sugawara handed me an expensive-looking set of his-and-hers chopsticks, telling me: "It's also a wedding gift." And the girls on the evening shift gave me a can of cookies.

Over the course of eighteen years I'd seen any number of people leaving, and in no time at all the gap they left was filled. The space I had occupied, too, would quickly be replenished, and from tomorrow the convenience store would carry on operating as usual.

I would never again be touching the tools of the trade I knew so well—the bar code scanner, the machine for placing orders, the mop for polishing the floor, the alcohol for disinfecting hands, the duster I'd always carried stuck through my belt.

"But still, it's an auspicious departure!" the manager said.

"It is!" Mrs. Izumi and Sugawara nodded. "Do come back to see us, won't you?"

"Yes, yes—do come back as a customer anytime. Bring Shiraha with you. We'll treat you to frankfurters."

Mrs. Izumi and Sugawara were smiling and wishing me luck.

I was taking on the form of a person that their brains all imagined as normal. Being congratulated by them felt strange, but I merely said, "Thank you."

I said goodbye to the girls on the evening shift and went outside. It was still light out, but the convenience store was lit up more brightly than the sky. It looked like a shining white aquarium.

I couldn't imagine what would become of me now I was no longer a store worker. I bowed once to the store and started walking to the metro station.

* * *

I got home to find Shiraha waiting impatiently for me.

Normally I would be concerned about work the next day and would be sure to care for my physical needs with food and sleep. My body had belonged to the convenience store even when I wasn't at work. Having been liberated from this, I didn't know what to do with myself.

Shiraha was in high spirits, checking the online help wanted ads. Résumé forms were scattered all around him on the living room table.

"A lot of jobs have an age limit, but there are some without if you look for them. I always hated looking at the ads, but since it isn't me that has to work, it's actually quite fun for once!"

I felt depressed. I looked at the clock: 7:00 p.m. My body had always been connected to the convenience store even when I wasn't working. Now it was time for the store's stock of carton drinks to be replenished; now the store's nighttime delivery would be arriving and the night shift would start checking it; now it was time for the store to have its floor mopped. Every time I looked at the clock, I would think about what was happening in the convenience store.

Now Sawaguchi from the evening shift would start making a POP ad for next week's new products, while Makimura topped up the cup noodle shelves. But I was now left out of that flow of time I thought.

There were numerous sounds in the apartment, from Shiraha's voice to the hum of the refrigerator, but my ears heard only silence. The sounds of the convenience store that had previously filled me to overflowing had now left my body. I was cut off from the world.

"Naturally, your job in a convenience store isn't enough to support me. With you working there and me jobless, I'm the one they'll criticize. Society hasn't dragged itself out of the Stone Age yet, and they'll always blame the man. But if you could just get a proper job, Furukura, they won't victimize me anymore and it'll be good for you, too, so we'd be killing two birds with one stone."

"Um, I haven't got any appetite today, so can you go get yourself something to eat?"

"What? Oh, okay then."

He grumbled about having to do the shopping himself, but he went quiet after I handed him a thousand-yen note.

That night I went to bed as usual but couldn't sleep, so I got up again and, still in my pajamas, went out onto the balcony.

Until now I had always needed to make sure I got enough sleep before work the next day. All I had to do was recall how I had to keep in shape for the sake of the convenience store and I would fall asleep right away, but now I didn't even know why I needed to sleep at all.

I always hung my laundry up to dry inside the apartment, so the balcony was dirty and mold was forming on the windows. I sat down anyway, not caring about my pajamas getting dirty.

I glanced back through the apartment window and saw the clock inside: 3:00 a.m., about the time the night shift took a break. Dat-kun and Shinozaki, a college student who'd started last week and had work experience from a previous store, would be using the time on their break to restock the walk-in refrigerator.

It was a long time since I'd been up at this hour.

I stroked my body. My nails were kept short as per store rules, and I was scrupulous about keeping my hair clean and had never dyed it. There was a faint scar on the back of my hand from when I burned myself while frying croquettes three days ago.

Summer might have been approaching, but it was still a bit chilly out on the balcony. But I didn't feel like going back inside, so I stayed outside, gazing blankly up at the indigo sky.

*   *   *

I awoke from a fitful sleep tossing and turning in the heat and opened my eyes a crack as I lay there in bed.

I had no idea what time it was, or even which day of the week. I fumbled around my pillow for my cell phone to check the time: two o'clock. Unable to grasp in my befuddled state whether it was morning or night, I climbed out of the closet. When I saw daylight coming in through the curtains, I finally registered it must be two in the afternoon.

I checked the date and realized that almost two weeks had passed since I'd stopped working at the convenience store. It felt like a long time ago, but also as though time had stopped.

Shiraha wasn't home. Maybe he'd gone out shopping for food. On the folding table, which had been left out, were the remains of the cup noodles we'd eaten yesterday.

Since I'd left the store, I no longer knew what time I should wake up in the morning. I slept whenever I felt sleepy and ate when I woke up. I didn't do anything all day except fill out résumé forms, as ordered by Shiraha.

I no longer knew what standard to live by. Until now, my body had belonged to the convenience store, even when I wasn't working. Sleeping, keeping in good physical shape, and eating nutritiously were all part of my job. I had to stay healthy for work.

Shiraha still slept in the bathtub, and during the day he came into the living room for his meals and to go through the help wanted ads. He seemed to be going about life with more energy than when I'd been working. I now spent all day and night in my bed inside the closet, only coming out when I felt hungry and never bothering to put the futon bedding away.

I realized I was thirsty. Mechanically I turned the faucet to fill a glass with water and drank it down in one go. I suddenly recalled hearing once that the water in a person's body was replaced every two weeks. It occurred to me that the water I used to buy every morning in the convenience store had already run through my body. The moisture in my skin, in the membrane over my eyeballs was probably no longer formed by the water from the convenience store.

Jet black hairs were sprouting on the fingers of my hand holding the glass and on my arms too. Until now I'd always been scrupulous over my personal appearance for the sake of the convenience store, but now that it was no longer necessary I didn't feel the need to shave. I looked in the mirror that stood in the living room and saw I had a faint moustache too.

Once every three days or so, when Shiraha insisted, I reluctantly went to the same coin-operated shower I'd previously used every day.

I had judged everything on the basis of whether it was the sensible thing to do for the convenience store, but now I'd lost that standard. There was nothing to guide me over whether an action was rational or not. Before I became a store worker, I must have been following some kind of logic in my judgments, but I'd forgotten whatever guiding principles I'd followed back then.

Suddenly I heard an electronic buzz, and I turned to see Shiraha's cell phone ringing on the tatami. He must have left it behind when he went out. I thought of just letting it ring, but it kept going on and on.

Wondering whether there was some kind of emergency, I looked at the screen and saw the words "Wife from Hell." Feeling a hunch I pressed ANSWER and sure enough the voice on the other end was that of his sister-in-law.

"How many times do I have to tell you?" she yelled. "I know where you are, and I'll butt in on you whenever I damn well like!"

"Um, hello. This is Furukura."

When she realized it was me on the phone, she immediately calmed down and said coolly, "Oh, it's you, is it?"

"Shiraha's out at the moment. He probably went to buy some food. I'm sure he'll be back right away."

"You'll do fine. Can I ask you to pass on a message about the loan to my brother-in-law? I haven't heard anything from him since he paid three thousand yen last week. What the hell is that? Three thousand yen! Barely enough to cover lunch for two. Is he taking the piss?"

"Oh. Er, I'm sorry." I stammered out apologetically.

"Look, pull yourself together. I have his signature on the IOU and I'll take him to court if I have to! Please tell him that, okay?" she said, clearly annoyed.

"Yes, I'll tell him as soon as he comes home."

"Make sure you do! The man is really greedy when it comes to money, I swear."

In the background, I heard the sound of a baby crying.

It suddenly occurred to me that no longer having the convenience store manual to follow, perhaps I should use animal instinct as the standard on which to base my judgments. I'm an animal of the human species so perhaps having children to make my species prosper would be the correct path for me.

"Um, may I ask you something? Is having children good for humanity?"

"What?"

She sounded so taken aback on the other end of the line that I thought I'd better explain what I meant.

"After all, we're animals, so isn't it better for our species if we multiply? Do you think it would be best for me and Shiraha to quickly get on with mating and play our part in making humanity prosper?"

For a while she was so quiet I thought she'd maybe hung up, but then I heard the sound of such a long, heavy sigh that I could almost feel her warm breath spewing out through the receiver.

"Give me a break! How do you think a store worker and an unemployed good-for-nothing are going to be able to raise children? Please don't even consider it. You'll be doing us all a favor by not leaving your genes behind. That's the best contribution to the human race you could make."

"Oh, really?"

"Keep those rotten genes to yourself for the course of your lifetime and take them to heaven with you when you die without leaving even a trace of them here on earth. Seriously."

"I see," I said nodding to myself, impressed at her ability to think so rationally.

"I swear that talking with you makes me feel dizzy. Plus it's a waste of time, so I'm going to say goodbye now. Oh, and make sure you tell him about the money, okay?" she said and hung up.

So apparently it would be better for the human race if Shiraha and I didn't mate. Since I'd never had sex and the very thought of it was ghastly, I was quite relieved about this. I would carry my genes carefully to my grave, being sure not to rashly leave any behind, and I would dispose of them properly when I died. I was resolved on this, but at the same time it left me in a bit of a limbo. I understood the end point perfectly, but how was I to spend my time until then?

I heard the door open, and Shiraha came in. He was carrying a plastic bag from a nearby hundred-yen shop. Now that my daily rhythm had been disrupted I rarely boiled vegetables for our feed, and instead he'd started buying frozen meals from the hundred-yen shop.

"Oh, you woke up?"

Even though we were both living in this small apartment, it had been some time since we'd last sat down to lunch together. The rice cooker was always left on, and my life revolved around waking up and shoving some rice into my mouth before getting back into my closet and sleeping again.

Having for once run into each other, we somehow ended up having lunch together. Shiraha defrosted some steamed dumplings and chicken nuggets and piled them onto plates. Wordlessly I put some in my mouth.

I didn't know what I was taking in nutrition for. I chewed the rice and dumplings to a pulp, but I couldn't bring myself to swallow.

*   *   *

Today I was going to my first interview. It was only for a temping agency, but for someone like me—a thirty-six-year-old woman who'd only ever worked in a convenience store—just managing to get an interview was nothing short of a miracle Shiraha told me, looking jubilant. Almost a month had passed since I'd resigned from the convenience store.

I was wearing a trouser suit I hadn't touched since having had it cleaned over ten years ago and had tied my hair back. It was the first time I'd left the apartment in quite a while too. The money I'd saved while working at the convenience store, meager as it was, had been considerably depleted.

"Well then, Furukura, let's get going."

Shiraha said he'd see me to the interview and was dead set on waiting for me outside until it was over.

We went out of the apartment into the hot, humid summer air and headed for the station. It was the first time I'd been on a train in quite a while too.

"We're a bit too early. There's still over an hour to go," Shiraha said when we arrived.

"Is there?"

"I'm just going to take a leak. Wait for me here," he said and walked off.

I wondered whether there was a public toilet nearby, but then saw that he'd gone into a convenience store. I should go to the toilet too, I thought and ran after him. As the automatic door slid open, I heard the familiar chimes.

"Irasshaimasé!" a girl behind the till called out as I walked in.

There was a queue to pay. I looked at the clock and saw it was almost noon. The lunchtime rush was just getting under way.

There were just two young women behind the counter, one wearing a badge that said: IN TRAINING. Both were frantically ringing up items on each of the two tills.

This was apparently a business district, since the customers all seemed to be either men in suits or young women who looked like office assistants.

And then the store's voice began streaming into me. All its sounds quivered with meaning, the vibrations speaking directly to my cells, like music to my ears. I knew instinctively what this store needed without even having to think about it.

I was startled to see the open refrigerated display case with an ad announcing 30¥ OFF ALL PASTA! The pasta dishes were all jumbled in with the yakisoba and okonomiyaki and didn't stand out at all.

This wouldn't do I thought, and I moved them to a more conspicuous spot next to the Korean-style cold noodles. A customer stared at me warily, but when I looked up and said "Irasshaimasé!" she appeared satisfied that I was a store employee and took one of the packs of spicy cod roe pasta I had just neatly laid out.

Perfect, I thought to myself, then immediately noticed the chocolates display. Hastily I took out my cell phone and checked the date. Today was Tuesday, new products day. How could the store workers have forgotten this, the single most important day in the week for a store?

I almost screamed when I saw there was only a single row of a new line of chocolates on the very lowest shelf. This was outrageous! It wasn't the way to display a limited seasonal white chocolate flavor of the very chocolates that six months ago had been such a huge hit and major best-selling product. I quickly rearranged the display, putting the sweets that didn't sell so well into a single row to free up space on the top shelf for three rows of the new line. Then I moved the NEW PRODUCT! label to draw attention to it.

One of the women on the tills was eyeing me suspiciously. She could see what I was doing, but she was busy attending to the queue of customers, unable to move. I made a gesture as if to show a badge on my breast and called out "Good morning!" taking care to not say it loud enough to disturb the customers.

Apparently reassured, she bowed slightly and went back to working the till. I was wearing a suit, so she probably thought I was from head office. Being so easily duped showed poor security I thought. What if I were a crook and opened the back room safe or stole money from the till?

I was making a mental note to warn her about that when I heard: "Hey, look! There's a white chocolate version of this out now." I looked around to see a couple of women picking up handfuls of new product I had just rearranged. "I saw an ad for this on TV just this morning. I have to try it now!"

A convenience store is not merely a place where customers come to buy practical necessities, it has to be somewhere they can enjoy and take pleasure in discovering things they like. I nodded in satisfaction and walked briskly around the store checking the displays.

It was a hot day, yet the stock of mineral water in the fridge was low. There was only one inconspicuously placed two-liter carton of barley tea out too, although these always sold well in hot weather.

I could hear the store's voice telling me what it wanted, how it wanted to be. I understood it perfectly.

There was a break in the queue, and the girl behind the till came running over to me. "Wow, that's amazing. It's like magic!" she whispered, gazing at the display of crisps I'd just arranged. "One of our part-timers didn't come in today. I tried to get in touch with the manager but I couldn't get through and was at my wit's end being on my own with just one new hire . . ."

"Is that what happened? But from what I can see, you're doing just fine." I said. "You're polite with the customers and were doing everything right on the till. Once the lunchtime rush is over, be sure to put out some nice cold drinks. And now that it's so hot, you'd better rearrange the ice-cream cabinet. Refreshing ice pops sell really well in this weather, so you'll need to put out some more of those. And the sundries shelf is a bit dusty. Take everything off it and give it a good clean."

I couldn't stop hearing the store telling me the way it wanted to be, what it needed. It was all flowing into me. It wasn't me speaking. It was the store. I was just channeling its revelations from on high.

"Yes, I'll do that," the girl said, her voice absolutely trusting.

"And the automatic door is covered in fingerprints. They really stand out, so you'd better give it a clean too. Also, you have a lot of women customers, so you should put a wider variety of cellophane noodle soup dishes out. Please be sure to tell the manager. And also—"

I was still relaying the store's voice to the store worker when someone shouted, "What the hell's going on here?" and grabbed my wrist. It was Shiraha, who had just come out of the bathroom.

"Excuse me, but what appears to be the problem?" I responded reflexively, as if to a customer.

"Stop taking the piss!" he shouted and dragged me out of the store onto the street. "Are you crazy? Just what do you think you're doing?"

"Listening to the voice of the convenience store." The thin pale skin covering his face crumpled in an expression of disgust, but I didn't back down. "The voice of the convenience store won't stop flowing through me. I was born to hear this voice."

"What the—" He was beginning to look scared.

"I realize now," I went on relentlessly. "More than a person, I'm a convenience store worker. Even if that means I'm abnormal and can't make a living and drop down dead, I can't escape that fact. My very cells exist for the convenience store."

His face was still scrunched up as he tugged on my wrist, evidently still determined to take me to the interview. "You're out of your mind. The village mentality of society will never permit such a creature to exist. It goes against the rules! You'll just be persecuted by everyone and live a lonely life. You'd be far better off working to support me. That way everyone'll breathe easier. They'll be satisfied. They'll even be happy for you."

"No, I can't go with you. Think of me as an animal, a convenience store animal. I can't betray my instinct."

"They'll never let you do it!"

I pulled myself up straight and faced him squarely, the way I did when uttering the store pledge in the morning ritual, and I said, "No. It's not a matter of whether they permit it or not. It's what I am. For the human me, it probably is convenient to have you around, Shiraha, to keep my family and friends off my back. But the animal me, the convenience store worker, has absolutely no use for you whatsoever."

I was wasting time talking like this. I had to get myself back in shape for the sake of the store. I had to restructure my body so it would be able to move more swiftly and precisely to replenish the refrigerated drinks or clean the floor, to more perfectly comply with the store's demands.

"That's grotesque. You're not human!" he spat.

That's what I've been trying to tell you! I thought. I finally managed to pull my hand from his grip and hugged it to my chest. That hand was important for giving customers their change and for wrapping their food orders. It felt disgustingly sticky from Shiraha's sweat and I wanted to wash it as soon as I possibly could. It was discourteous to customers to leave it like this!

"You'll regret this. Mark my words!" Shiraha shouted as he walked off alone back to the station.

I took my mobile out of my bag. First I needed to call the company that was interviewing me to tell them I wouldn't be attending because I was a convenience store worker. And then I had to find a new store to work in.

I caught sight of myself reflected in the window of the convenience store I'd just come out of. My hands, my feet—they existed only for the store! For the first time, I could think of the me in the window as a being with meaning.

"Irasshaimasé!"

I thought of the window in the hospital where I first saw my newborn nephew. Through the reflection a bright voice resembling mine rang out. I could distinctly feel all my cells stirring within my skin as they responded in unison to the music reverberating on the other side of the glass.

Read on for an essay by Sayaka Murata,
translated by Ginny Tapley Takemori,
which first appeared in *Literary Hub*
on June 14, 2018.

Dear Convenience Store,

I hope you don't mind me getting straight to the point. We've known each other for seventeen years, but I guess this is the first time I've ever written you a letter.

I was eighteen when we met. I thought you were really scary to begin with. You were so grown up, and I thought you wouldn't have time for the likes of me. I always felt nervous with you, and I kept a notebook in my pocket to jot down detailed notes on every little gesture or habit of yours as I noticed them.

I don't suppose either of us could pinpoint the exact moment we fell in love. If I had to hazard a guess, I would probably say it was that night when were together at 2 a.m. for the first time. Somebody had suddenly called in sick and begged me to cover for them, so I was left inside you until the middle of the night. I'd only ever met you during the day or evening, and I was thrilled by the scent of the summer's night on the air that came flowing into you.

When it was time to go home, I suddenly had the urge to see you look embarrassed, so I asked, "Do you think a convenience store and a human can have sex together?" thinking it would make you blush and get all flustered. But you answered smoothly, your face utterly serious, "What are you talking about? We're already doing it, aren't we? You enter me every day." I think that's the moment we became lovers.

Since then I don't go to work—I go on dates, all dressed up for the occasion. And you too greet me a little cockily with your magazine racks and store mirrors sparkling clean.

It did occur to me that by the same logic you must be having sex with everyone from the geezer on the night shift to the couple who are your managers and hundreds of customers, but when I put this to you, you answered unhesitatingly, "What? But I've only ever done it with you!" so I suppose there must be something different for you.

It must have been about three years after I met you that I was told you were going to die in a month's time. I was so shocked I couldn't speak. I'd never thought a convenience store would live for only three years.

But you really did die. For two days before your death, everything in you was reduced to half price, and people flocked in to buy it all up. All I could think of as I watched them was that I'd never be able to see you again.

I was taken aback, then, when the managers told me you were going to be reborn a fifteen-minute bicycle ride away. It was the first time I'd ever dated a convenience store, so I never knew that it was in your nature to repeatedly die and be reborn.

I fell in love all over again with the reborn you. We had our ups and downs, like my affair with a family restaurant, and your dying again. By the third time you died, though, I'd gotten used to it. And even now, after seventeen years of splitting up and getting back together again, we're still together.

"There are so many things I love about you that even a hundred pages wouldn't be enough to cover them all."

People say things like, "Why are you dating a convenience store? Doesn't it matter that it's not human?" and "It's been ages now, aren't you fed up with it yet?" and "There's no way that's true love. You must be doing it to get material for your next novel."

I'm used to it and don't give it a second thought, but when I brought it up half jokingly on a date recently, you looked a little sad. "I'm sorry, I shouldn't have told you. Shall I kill the people who said those kinds of things?" I asked, only half kidding. "Oh no, you mustn't do that," you answered, completely serious. "They won't come back to life like I do."

Now that I think about it, it's rare for you to show any emotion. You never really laugh even when I tell a joke, and if I suddenly rub up against you intimately, you always keep your cool and never go red. But I always believed that you knew why I loved you, even if I didn't spell it out for you. And yet the other day, when we were splitting up for the nth time and ended up arguing for ages, you suddenly blurted out, "I still don't even know why you're going out with me."

That really shocked me. And it's because I want you to understand that I'm writing to you now.

There are so many things I love about you that even a hundred pages wouldn't be enough to cover them all, so I'll give you just one concise reason.

The number one reason I love you is that you made me human.

Everyone goes on about how you're not human, but until I met you I was the non-human one. At least

I wasn't the sort of human who could function well as one. But that changed, thanks to being with you.

You gave me the flow of time, with morning, afternoon, and night, and the gift of miraculous shoes to walk around the real world. For me you were a magician. Without you, I would probably have lived my life without ever being aware that a period of time called morning even existed.

You were the sole unshakable "normal" in my life, and so my feelings as a human are all yours.

But I'm getting kind of heavy here, aren't I? Maybe we really are going to split up once and for all. Love has turned me into that weird creature called a human, but you will never be anything but a convenience store. Maybe my devotion has become a bit of a drag for you.

I wonder about what it will mean to lose you. Without you, I will probably forget how to be human again. Being that dependent on you is kind of scary.

But let's stay together a little longer. I know you're not without your faults: you're showing signs of wear and tear here and there; the endless ding-dong of your door chime gets on my nerves after a while; our dates are always in the same place since you say you can't go anywhere, being a building; the food you're so proud of having cooked yourself is full of additives; and you give me extra work by suddenly introducing a coffee machine and telling me, "Look! Look! A new toy!" And apart from anything else, the geezer on the night shift and the managers enter your body and wriggle around to their hearts' content—how is that not being unfaithful? But then, I can't help finding your faults charming too, so my love for you must be an illness. Frankly, I think it's your duty to stay with me until I'm cured of it.

We'll be having another date tomorrow morning. Lately I've been just going through the motions and wearing the same old jeans all the time, but tomorrow I'll wear a brand new dress. I want you to dress up for me, too. Make sure you're super clean, even inside your backroom refrigerator, okay?

Come to think of it, we've never even kissed. Let's make tomorrow the day we have our first kiss.

Yours,
Sayaka Murata